A WATE

Touch the Sky felt himsel... ...g swung, heaved. Then he hit the ice-cold water. Unable to kick, he swam desperately with one arm barely keeping his chin out of the water. Another splash nearby told him Little Horse, too, had been thrown in.

''Look at the odd fishes!'' a Cherokee warrior taunted. ''Are they trout with braids?''

''No, they are Cheyenne warrior fish!''

Touch the Sky neared the bank slowly, but it was impossible to swim straight with only one arm. He was immediately seized and thrown back out into midstream. Little Horse received similar treatment.

Over and over he and Little Horse made it close to shore only to be tossed back in. Now his arm was so weak it felt heavy as a stone club, and he was swallowing more and more water. The merciless taunts continued although by now he heard little in his desperate struggle to stay alive.

As Touch the Sky was lifted and swung, be began chanting his death song....

12 CHEYENNE

MANKILLER
JUDD COLE

Northeast MO Library
207 W. Chestnut St.
Kahoka, MO 63445

LEISURE BOOKS　　　NEW YORK CITY

A LEISURE BOOK®

December 1994

Published by

Dorchester Publishing Co., Inc.
276 Fifth Avenue
New York, NY 10001

If you purchased this book without a cover you should be aware
that this book is stolen property. It was reported as ''unsold and
destroyed'' to the publisher and neither the author nor the publisher
has received any payment for this ''stripped book.''

Copyright © 1994 by Dorchester Publishing Co., Inc.

All rights reserved. No part of this book may be reproduced or
transmitted in any form or by any electronic or mechanical means,
including photocopying, recording or by any information storage
and retrieval system, without the written permission of the Publisher,
except where permitted by law.

The name ''Leisure Books'' and the stylized ''L'' with design are
trademarks of Dorchester Publishing Co., Inc.

Printed in the United States of America.

Prologue

In the year the white man's winter count called 1840, a Northern Cheyenne infant was the sole survivor of a bluecoat ambush on his band near the North Platte. His Cheyenne name lost forever, he was adopted by white parents in the Wyoming river-bend settlement of Bighorn Falls.

John and Sarah Hanchon named the boy Matthew and raised him as if he were their own. He grew to be a tall, broad-shouldered youth with the even and pleasing looks that had earned the Cheyenne tribe the name of the Beautiful People among their red brothers. There were constant reminders of the fear and mistrust many settlers felt toward an Indian in their midst. But his parents were good to him, as were his young friend Corey Robinson and the former mountain man called Old Knobby. Matthew grew up sensing something was wrong, but nonetheless feeling accepted in his limited world.

Then came his sixteenth year and the tragedy that would leave him an outcast. When the wealthy rancher Hiram Steele caught his daughter Kristen with Matthew in their secret meeting place, Steele ordered one of his wranglers to viciously beat Matthew. He also warned the hapless youth that if he caught them together again, he would kill the Cheyenne. Fearing for Matthew's life, Kristen lied and told him she never wanted to see him again.

Hard upon the heels of this followed more trouble. Seth Carlson, a cavalry officer stationed at nearby Fort Bates, had staked a claim to Kristen. To Matthew's misery Carlson added a threat. If Matthew didn't clear out of Bighorn Falls for good, Carlson would destroy the Hanchon's contract to supply Fort Bates, which was the main reason why their mercantile business was flourishing.

Rejected by the white world, and fearful of hurting his adopted parents by staying, Matthew hardened his heart for whatever lay ahead. Then he left Bighorn Falls forever and fled north to the Powder River country of the Northern Cheyenne. But he quickly discovered that the red man, too, feared and mistrusted him. Captured by braves from Chief Yellow Bear's camp, he was declared a spy for the whites and sentenced to torture and death.

A wily, hotheaded young brave named Wolf

Mankiller

Who Hunts Smiling was on the verge of gutting Matthew when Arrow Keeper interceded. The tribe's medicine man and keeper of the sacred Medicine Arrows, Arrow Keeper had recently been to Medicine Lake, where a great and epic vision was placed over his eyes. This vision prophesied the arrival of a young stranger—the long-lost son of a great Cheyenne chief named Running Antelope. This stranger would someday lead the Cheyenne people in their last great struggle for freedom. But he would also be doomed to suffer many hardships before he could lift high the lance of leadership.

Arrow Keeper discovered the mark of the warrior buried past Matthew's hairline, and that sign convinced him the youth was the same war leader of his medicine dream. But Wolf Who Hunts Smiling was outraged when Arrow Keeper's interference spared the prisoner's life. So was his older cousin, the stern, young war leader Black Elk, who was jealous of the glances exchanged between Matthew and Honey Eater, Chief Yellow Bear's unmarried daughter. Many others, too, were angered when Arrow Keeper announced that the accused spy would not only be spared from execution—he would live with the tribe and train under Black Elk as a warrior!

Arrow Keeper buried Matthew's white name forever in a hole, renaming the tall youth Touch the Sky. In the beginning, his fate seemed hopeless. Hated and scorned, called Woman Face and White Man's Dog, he could not ride bareback, hunt buffalo, or even aim a throwing ax. Adding to his grief, Wolf Who Hunts Smiling walked between Touch the Sky and the campfire—the Cheyenne way of announcing his intention to kill the tall stranger.

Then Chief Yellow Bear's camp fell under attack by a vastly superior Pawnee force. Teaming up with his new friend Little Horse, Touch the Sky managed to use white man's trickery to frighten away the superstitious Pawnees and save his tribe. He was honored in a special council, but such recognition only further hardened his enemies—especially Wolf Who Hunts Smiling and Black Elk—against him.

Thus began his long and bitter struggle for acceptance. He faced Henri Lagace and his murderous whiskey peddlers; Wes Munro and his well-armed land-grabbers; Kiowas and Comanches and Comanchero slave traders; Seth Carlson and his Indian-killing regiment; the crazy-by-thunder renegade Blackfoot Siski-dee; white buffalo hiders and the vindictive Comanche war leader Big Tree. Through all this he developed into a warrior worth five braves.

Arrow Keeper, recognizing Touch the Sky's gift of visions, selected him to be the tribe's next shaman and Keeper of the Arrows. Yet, his Cheyenne enemies cleverly turned appearances against him, planted damaging rumors, and otherwise intrigued to keep many in the tribe suspicious of him.

Forced to marry Black Elk when her father died, Honey Eater still loved only Touch the Sky. Black Elk's jealous wrath could have exploded at any moment, leading him to kill either or both of them. And numerous enemies outside the tribe, red men, soldiers, and hair-face settlers, were eager to lift Touch the Sky's scalp.

Chapter One

"Brothers!" the young brave called Tangle Hair shouted. "Look to the north. Thunder Bonnet is flashing a signal!"

Tangle Hair sat his pony on a grassy rise between the Powder River and the many clan circles of Chief Gray Thunder's camp. Below him a group of young braves sat in the new grass, fashioning arrow shafts from green oak and chipping points out of flintstones. Among them were Touch the Sky, Little Horse, Two Twists, and several of Tangle Hair's troop brothers from the Bow String Soldier Society.

Touch the Sky was by far the tallest and broadest in the shoulders, muscled more like the Apaches to the southwest than a typical slender-limbed Plains warrior of the north country. Like his companions he had recently abandoned his leggings and leather shirt as the warm moons took over. All wore soft doeskin clouts, elkskin moccasins, wide leather bands around their left wrists to protect them from the sharp slap of bow strings.

Touch the Sky and his companions rose and looked toward the serried peaks of the Bighorn Mountains. Day and night a sentry was kept posted there on the high benchland between the mountains and the confluence of the Powder and Little Powder, site of Chief Gray Thunder's summer camp. The sentry always kept a fragment of mirror to flash signals back into the valley on sunny days.

"Tangle Hair, call his message out for us," Touch the Sky said. "From here we cannot see over the tipis."

Others in camp, too, had seen the signals. The word spread through the Indian village like grassfire in a windstorm. Cheyennes frustrated their enemies by keeping many dogs for security; upset by the unusual activity, they were raising a howling, barking clamor. Any message from a sentry was important and meant someone was approaching. But was it friend or foe?

Tangle Hair shaded his eyes with one hand. He squinted into the brassy glow on the horizon, where a late afternoon sun reflected off rock spires and endless veins of mica and quartz and feldspar.

The clamor of excited dogs and ponies and children was too loud to shout above. Touch the Sky watched his friend pull a finger across his forehead, signifying the brim of a hat.

"White men approach," he said to his friends, translating Tangle Hair's sign language.

Touch the Sky's words brought a sense of urgency to the faces of his companions. Their Sioux cousins had spent a miserable winter fighting white soldiers and militiamen in the Black Hills. It was rumored the whiteskins were ready to subdue the Cheyennes and force them to accept a reservation far from this place.

"But these whiteskins come in peace," Touch the Sky said, watching Tangle Hair lift two empty hands toward them. "It is a caravan bringing our talking-paper goods!"

A cheer rose throughout camp as others farther up the bank translated out loud. This was indeed an important event. The cold moons had been hard. Long had the people huddled over the firepits in their tipis, depleting their supplies of meat, flour, tobacco, and sugar. The arrival of this caravan meant the end of much suffering, a chance to let the winter-starved ponies graze and fatten for the hunts to come.

"Look there," Little Horse said, pointing across the vast central clearing toward the circle where the Panther Clan pitched their tipis. As was the custom, each entrance faced east to the rising sun. "Wolf Who Hunts Smiling and Black Elk hurry to rig their horses and ride out. Like bully coyotes snatching the red meat, they want to make first claim to the best goods."

"In this they show many faces," Two Twists said bitterly.

He was the youngest of the group and named after his preference for wearing his hair in two braids instead of one. Under Touch the Sky, he had led the junior warriors in a successful defense against Kiowa and Comanche raiders. Like Little Horse, he was loyal to Touch the Sky, though many in the tribe called the tall brave a spy because he had been raised by whites and still had friends among the settlers and blue-bloused soldiers. To be his friend within the tribe was a risky business.

"They hurry for their share," Two Twists said, "yet they bellowed loudest when Touch the Sky agreed to be a pathfinder for the hair-face miners and their iron horse. They called Touch the Sky a white man's dog. They said Caleb Riley and his crew were thieves stealing the red homeland. They huffed up their chests, played the big Indians, and said they wanted no part of the profits."

"Now look," Little Horse said. "Carrion birds flocking to the kill."

Touch the Sky said nothing, though certainly his friends had truth firmly by the tail. He and Little Horse had risked their lives to earn this annual delivery of goods—goods which Black Elk, Wolf Who Hunts Smiling, and many of their brothers in the highly feared Bull Whip Soldier Society had sworn never to touch. Caleb, younger brother of the cavalry officer Tom Riley, had promised a consignment every year. This profit sharing would continue so long as his company transported their ore on a railroad spur line across Cheyenne hunting grounds to Laramie, where it was shipped back to the St. Louis settlements.

Judd Cole

"Thunder Bonnet adds more!" Tangle Hair
shouted. The clamor had quieted some and he
could be heard again. "The caravan will arrive
in the time it takes the sun to travel the width
of three lodge poles."

Suddenly a holiday mood prevailed throughout camp. Toothless old grandmothers smiled
wide, anticipating fine white sugar for their
yarrow tea; young women spoke excitedly of
new calico and linsey cloth for dresses; even
the stern-faced warriors grinned sheepishly at
each other, heartened by the prospect of folding
knives, moist brown tobacco, and bars of pig lead
for moulding new bullets.

Against his will, Touch the Sky let his gaze cut
to the finest tipi within the Panther Clan circle,
one boasting new hide covers and meat racks
out back—Black Elk's. And there, speaking to her
aunt, Sharp Nosed Woman, was Honey Eater.

Black Elk had ridden out, and Touch the Sky
knew it should be safe to look at her. But
long, careful habit made him slow to do so. In
matters pertaining to battle, Black Elk's mind
was usually clear and strong. But his jealousy
turned even a glance from another warrior into
an excuse to punish Honey Eater savagely. When
Touch the Sky's eyes found her, she was looking
his way.

They held each other for a long moment with
gazes of mutual need, unaware of anyone or
anything else. Their love had become such a
hunted, forbidden thing that moments like these
were as rare, pleasing, and disturbing to them as
stolen caresses. It was the great, unspoken secret

14

of village life. An old grandmother of the Sky Walker Clan had once sung their love to entertain the young girls. Since then, the verses had been sung over and over in the sewing lodge.

But when Touch the Sky spotted one of Black Elk's friends from the Bull Whip's staring at him, he turned away and avoided Honey Eater. Black Elk flew into rages against his squaw at the slightest excuse. It had been an important moment in their love when Honey Eater had told Touch the Sky she considered him her only husband—that she would come to him and lie beside him if he sent for her. But it was a moment important for the offer, not the possibility of doing it—certainly not while Black Elk was alive.

Many had mounted their ponies and ridden out to meet the caravan. The lead horses and mules were visible, skirting around the benchland through widely scattered cotton-woods. The white men conducting the train were a hard, dirty lot—unshaven men with long, lanky hair hanging loose or tied in knots under broad-brimmed hats.

As the pack animals filed into camp, panniers and pack saddles bulging, braves from the soldier societies were forced to keep the excited people back. The Bow Strings patiently sidestepped their ponies and nudged the people back; the Bull Whips, in contrast, resorted to their whips, making them hiss and crack and even raising a few welts on those who moved too slow.

"H'ar now! Git the hell back, you red niggers!" the lead bull-whacker shouted in English.

15

"Move your flea-bit blanket asses, yuh heathen sonsabitches!"

Touch the Sky stepped close to him, one hand resting on the beaded sheath of his knife. "Next time you ride into a Cheyenne camp," he said in perfect English, "hold one palm up in peace, or kiss your sitter good-bye. Now leave the supplies and make tracks out of here. And if you insult my tribe one more time, I'll feed your guts to the dogs."

The bull-whacker stared, measuring not only the brave's considerable stature, but also the fierce, barely restrained hatred pulsing to be unleashed in quick and violent action.

Some in the tribe—encouraged by the constant talk of Wolf Who Hunts Smiling, Swift Canoe, and others—suspected Touch the Sky's English greeting was a mark of fawning, another proof he played the dog for whites. But this notion was quickly dispelled when the bull-whacker's eyes widened for a moment in fear.

Then he caged his eyes, much as the Indians themselves were doing.

"Whatever you say, John," he said, employing the name frontier whites always used in direct address to an Indian. "I'm more 'n happy to get shut of this load and clear out. I ain't one for spilling chin music with Injuns."

He shouted brief commands and soon the entire delivery of crates, bags, and kegs was heaped in the central clearing. The Cheyenne soldiers kept the people back while River of Winds—who was highly respected for his honesty—made a quick initial inspection.

The bull-whackers had turned the pack animals back toward the mountains with loud cracks of their own long whips. Abruptly, River of Winds called out.

"Hold!" Touch the Sky's shouted command in English halted the whiteskins.

River of Winds had just examined a huge slab of bacon, peeling back the layer of cheesecloth covering it. He looked from Chief Gray Thunder to both of the soldier chiefs, Spotted Tail of the Bow Strings and Lone Bear of the Bull Whips.

"Look here! Someone has played the fox."

River of Winds peeled the outer slab back. Packed under the cheesecloth were several large, flat stones.

"And look here," he said to Touch the Sky, pointing at a big hunk of salt pork. "Never before has the meat had these odd blue symbols on it. What do they mean?"

Touch the Sky peered closer and read the words stamped on the meat: *Condemned For Troop Use.*

"And here," River of Winds said, "look at the blankets. Somehow they are different."

Suddenly the camp was filled with indignant outcries. An old woman who recognized the shiny surface of shoddy-and-glue blankets stepped forward with a gourd full of water. She poured it on one of the blankets, then easily pulled it apart.

"This," she said bitterly, "is what happens to them in the first rain. We were given wagonloads of these after all the chiefs signed the talking papers at the soldiertown called Fort Laramie."

The bull-whackers spoke no Cheyenne. But clearly things were turning ugly. They bunched tighter together as angry braves began to form a dangerous wall around them.

"H'ar now!" the leader said. He looked at Touch the Sky and pulled a sheaf of papers out of his sash. "You talk good English, John. Read 'er, too?"

Touch the Sky nodded. The other thrust the papers toward him.

"That's mighty providential, then. 'Cuz iffen you glom over that paper, you'll see for certain that we ain't got squat to do with this here consignment 'cept to deliver it. We done that. I'm a freighter, not a supplier. Who you want to chew it fine with is whoever owns the Frontier Supply Company in the Kansas Territory."

At this point Black Elk stepped forward from a knot of warriors. His face was stern with anger. The effect was made even more fearsome by the leathery hunk where one ear had been severed by a bluecoat saber. Black Elk had killed the soldier, then sewn the ear back onto his skull with buckskin thread after the battle.

"These whiteskins tried to cheat us," he told Touch the Sky angrily. "No more secret councils with them in the hair-face tongue as you are doing now. Tell them to produce our goods, or we Bull Whip troopers will exact the value from their hides."

When Black Elk cracked his whip and several of his troop brothers followed suit, Touch the Sky felt a familiar trap closing on him again. Everyone was staring at him, waiting for him

18

to prove his loyalty to the Cheyenne people once and for all. Yet this disgusting freighter with lice in his beard had a legitimate point: There was certainly no proof they were behind the deliberate fraud.

"Father," he said, turning directly to Gray Thunder, "this place hears what I say! I, too, am enraged by this cruel crime. And I would speak with two tongues if I told you the lives of these dogs matter to me. No doubt they have shot more than one red man in his sleep. And no doubt they knew the supplies were worthless.

"But, Father, we have no proof that these hair faces robbed us. Indeed, if we punish them, the crime will then be treated as smoke behind us, and the true culprits will go unpunished to steal from red men again. I am for wading in a bit slower and seeing how deep we are in. We must try to get the goods that are owed to us."

Gray Thunder was a vigorous warrior with some 40 winters behind him. He was popular with his people, a strong believer in voicing the will of the tribe rather than trying to dictate it. He joined old Arrow Keeper and several of the headmen in nodding at the fairness and good sense of Touch the Sky's words.

"Fathers! Brothers! These are familiar and dangerous words!" Wolf Who Hunts Smiling said. "Do you remember how this one, this Touch the Sky, praised his paleface friend, Caleb Riley? 'Let the hair faces build a path for their iron horse across our hunting grounds,' he cried. 'They are friends to the red man,' this one insisted. 'They will make us rich.'

"But this day we see how our white friends treat us! The yellow beard, Caleb Riley, is behind this treachery. And now this pretend Cheyenne, whom I now openly call White Man Runs Him, once again coats the bitter truth with honey. He grew up wearing white man's shoes, and truly, he still walks in them despite his Indian moccasins."

By now the bull-whackers were too scared to go for their weapons—a move that would surely kill them, surrounded as they were. Showing this fear was their second mistake, especially in front of Black Elk.

"Truly my cousin speaks the straight word," Black Elk said. "These shivering cowards will die, and I will kill the first."

His obsidian blade had not quite cleared its sheath when Gray Thunder spoke up with unaccustomed sharpness.

"Black Elk, you are our war leader, and I never smoked the common pipe with a better one. But this is not a battle matter. Nor is this which you propose a battle—it is outright murder. Touch the Sky spoke straight arrow. For all we know, these white fools are no more guilty than the horses and mules that carried this worthless load. I say the whites will ride out unharmed."

"What if they are guilty?" Wolf Who Hunts Smiling said, backing his older cousin.

But it was old Arrow Keeper who spoke up. His voice was cracked and sere with age, even more with recent illness. But his words still resonated with great authority.

"What of that, buck? Many crimes go unde-
tected, do they not? For instance, some in
this tribe have attempted to kill a fellow
Cheyenne, spilling the blood of our own and
thus staining the sacred Medicine Arrows with
bloody dishonor. Indeed," Arrow Keeper said,
staring shrewdly at Wolf Who Hunts Smiling,
"some in this tribe, in their brutal quest for
power, may have shed the blood of our own
by huddling with our enemies. Yet they prate
about playing the big Indian and speaking of
Cheyenne honor."

Touch the Sky was sure he saw blood rush into
Wolf Who Hunts Smiling's face. Clearly Arrow
Keeper was hinting about Wolf Who Hunts Smiling's suspected collaboration with the Comanche
renegade, Big Tree—a crime Touch the Sky alone
had sure knowledge of. He had sworn, in front of
council, to kill Wolf Who Hunts Smiling for the
tribal blood he had shed.

But the hotheaded, wily Wolf Who Hunts
Smiling was never at a loss for words.

"And perhaps some others in this tribe, Grandfather," he said, stressing the last word with
great meaning, "have grown tangle brained and
thunderstruck in their frosted years, mistaking
shadows for enemies. Perhaps it is time for
younger bulls who see better to lead the herd."

An awkward silence followed this exchange of
remarks. But Gray Thunder's stern resolve never
wavered. Reluctant, but loath to rebel against
a peace chief he respected, Black Elk stepped
back and slipped his knife into the sheath.

"Very well. Let the white dogs flee with their

tails between their legs," he said. He joined his younger cousin in staring hard at Touch the Sky. "Once again this one has defended the people who raised him. He speaks of holding back now, of burying the hatchet in the interest of securing our goods.

"But only wait. Snow will blow into our tipis. The white men will be warm and fat, and we Cheyennes will be doing the hurt dance. This pretend Cheyenne will do nothing for us except help the whiteskins take our land and destroy our way of life!"

"I have had a vision placed over my eyes," Arrow Keeper said later that day. "It was sent by Maiyun, the Day Maker."

This abrupt announcement startled Touch the Sky. The two friends sat crosslegged on a pile of buffalo robes near the firepit of Arrow Keeper's tipi. It was still cool in the evenings, and a sagewood fire sent fragrant clouds curling out the tipi's smokehole.

"A vision, Father?"

"Yes. That is why I called you over. I will speak more about it in a few moments. It is true, is it not, that you plan to ride out after sunrise? You and Little Horse?"

Touch the Sky nodded, not at all surprised that Arrow Keeper knew this even before he told him. It was necessary to lean even closer to hear his old friend. In the dancing firelight, Touch the Sky noticed how deeply etched were the age lines crisscrossing the old shaman's face. His breathing was hard, often labored. Now and then the old man coughed into a piece of sack-cloth. Touch the Sky noticed bright red flecks of blood speckling the cloth.

"You are riding to the mining site to visit Caleb Riley?"

Touch the Sky nodded. "He is no thief, Father. Like his brother, Tom, he speaks only one way to the red man. But he may know something useful about this theft of our goods."

"He is a good man," Arrow Keeper said. "But there are many, like Black Elk and Wolf Who Hunts Smiling, who preach that no whites can be decent. And failing to understand that there are as many white men as there are blades of grass on the plains, these young Cheyenne hotheads are for exterminating all whites. They would find it easier to drink the Powder dry."

Arrow Keeper paused while a spasm of hard coughing racked his body. He fell quiet and stared long into the fire. Touch the Sky waited patiently, knowing the old shaman would eventually speak words of great importance to his destiny.

"Soon, stout buck, you and Little Horse will be up against it again. The battle will be hard. You will ride a great distance and find yourself in unfamiliar lands. An old enemy from your past is back—and he means to kill you."

Touch the Sky's mouth was a grim, determined slit. Arrow Keeper had spoken as if in a trance, and the words made Touch the Sky's palms throb.

"An old enemy, Father? Who?"

Still staring into the fire, his rheumy old eyes

aglow from the flames, Arrow Keeper shook his head.

"As always, there was much to my vision which the Powerful One did not mean for me to understand. But things are the way they are, and this much I can tell you."

Arrow Keeper looked at Touch the Sky, his eyes intense with urgency. When he spoke, he said words that did not seem to emanate from him, but from some higher power. Touch the Sky felt his nape tingle.

"Beware the man with an eagle's grip," Arrow Keeper said in the trance voice, "and be prepared to die before you are dead!"

These words baffled Touch the Sky and left him numb with confusion. When Arrow Keeper fell into a deep silence, unable to say more, Touch the Sky, long familiar with the mysterious old medicine man's ways, once again tasted the familiar, coppery taste of fear.

Chapter Two

In 1860 the vast Kansas Territory was a turmoiled region on the brink of statehood. Like other areas on the American frontier, it attracted many profiteering adventurers inspired by the acquisitive spirit of the times—those following the popular adage that the sun traveled west, and so did opportunity.

One growing source of windfall profits was the vast region known as the Indian Territory— huge tracts of land set aside by Congress as reservations for the Five Civilized Tribes forcibly relocated by the Removal Bill of 1830: the Seminoles, Cherokees, Chickasaws, Choctaws, and Creeks. Each tribe was promised regular payments of trade goods from the U. S. Government. Now certain white men, and their corrupt Indian lackeys, were making a fortune by routinely cheating the tribes.

For years Hiram Steele owned a successful mustang ranch near the Wyoming Territory settlement of Bighorn Falls—successful because he was ruthless and believed in destroying competition by whatever means it took.

But he had recently gone into the much more profitable enterprise of supplying contract goods to various Indian tribes. He had so far landed contracts—private and government—to supply tribes both on and off reservations: the still wild Cheyennes and Arapahos up north as well as the "dust scatterers" or "praying Indians" at the Great Bend Cherokee Reservation, presently his major source of lucrative contracts for services and goods.

In fact, Great Bend was so important to his growing empire that Steele had sold his ranch in Wyoming, pulled up stakes, and moved with his daughter Kristen to the small but thriving river town located on the western boundary of the Cherokee reservation, which bore the same name as the town. A few friendly meetings with the reservation agent, a professional bureaucrat from Virginia named Ephraim Long, had quickly evolved into a partnership that was making both men rich.

At the same time that Touch the Sky and Arrow Keeper were holding private council in the upcountry of the Powder, Hiram Steele was entertaining guests at his new home in Great Bend. They sat around a cloth-covered puncheon table, smoking cigars and sipping aged Scotch: Hiram Steele, Indian Agent Ephraim Long, and the Cherokee Chief called Red Jacket.

"Gentlemen," Steele said, carefully picking a speck of tobacco from his lip, "before we get down to cases, just a brief word of caution. The citizens of Great Bend were more than grateful when I donated the funds to employ selected Cherokees as a private police force for the reservation. But this brave you picked to head them, this—"

"His name is Mankiller," Long said. "An amazing tracker and woodsman."

"Among other things," Steele said dryly. "I'm concerned that you and the chief here aren't keeping a tight enough rein on him."

Red Jacket seemed to find this idea amusing, but he was polite and restrained his mirth to the silent abdomen laugh Indians employed to show restraint around whites.

"No one puts reins on a crazy grizzly," Red Jacket said, but the other two ignored him as usual.

"I hear rumors in town," Steele said. "Talk about a violent Cherokee constable, about Indians turning up dead. Don't forget, we started this police force to protect our interests, not to jeopardize them."

"Valid point," Long said. "But it was you who said you wanted a man as mean and hard as the job itself."

"I can't deny that. I also believe that money should be put to work making more money, which is the real point of this meeting. This side deal I recently concluded with the Far West Mining Company up north proved quite profitable. Panned out damn tidy, matter of fact. I supplied numerous trade items to some tribe of Northern Cheyennes. I was able to cut my expenses considerably by selecting the goods with thrift. Now I think it's time to put those profits to work generating more."

Steele's eyes had clouded with anger when he mentioned the Cheyennes. Ephraim Long noticed this and filed the fact away for later use. Now he grinned slightly at Steele's allusion to cutting expenses. The agent was a tall, slender man with muttonchop whiskers. He was a fastidious man and now wore a gray duster to protect his dark twill suit. He carried no weapon openly, but tucked into his right boot was a two-shot ladies muff pistol—so-called because wealthy women in London carried them in their muffs when passing through unsavory sections of the city.

"The way I see it," Long said, "those who teach the red man to plow and pray deserve some reward for their difficult labors. Just what have you got in mind, Hiram?"

Steele settled back in his chair and crossed his ankles. He was in his forties, with flint-gray eyes and a seamed face too stern to call handsome. The man was true to his name—hard and unbending, even his smile was rigid.

"Well now, I think maybe it's about time that you and Red Jacket thought about petitioning the Indian Bureau for a vocational school on the reservation. I hear that the Indian lovers in Congress like to fund vocational schools. They teach the younger ones something besides hunting and stealing. Someplace where the boys could learn how to tend a furnace or mend saddles, the girls how to sew and cook and what not. Whaddya say, Chief? That sound jake to you?"

Red Jacket helped himself to a little more whiskey from a glass carboy on the table. He was thoroughly civilized, as were many in his Cherokee tribe. He could read and write English, and he dressed in white man's clothing and called himself a Christian. Some of his people, however, called him a cracker-and-molasses chief: an Indian leader in name only who licked the white men's hands for crumbs and put himself before his tribe. His name derived from a pompous penchant for wearing red wool jackets tailored in the style of British military tunics.

"I am always ready to do what I can for our young people," he said piously. "True it is, the great white chief named Jefferson confused us by speaking two ways at once. First he sent us hoes and plows, telling us to cease being hunters. Then they found gold on our land, and the Great White Council praised the hunting further west, urging us to move here.

"And now, we are here. More than four thousand of us died during the journey. But have we rebelled and joined the heathen warriors of the Plains tribes as some Sacs and Foxes did? No! Only look. We are the sole tribe with a recorded language, the only reservation with its own newspaper. We wish to be like our white brothers, not to kill them. I am for this school. I—"

Judd Cole

"That's real nice, Chief," Steele said impatiently, cutting the loquacious Indian short. Once he started drinking, Red Jacket loved to hear himself talk. "You're a true credit to your tribe. Here, have another cigar. Take a few for later, too. That's it. Don't be bashful."

Red Jacket smiled wide and slipped several of the fine smokes into his pocket.

"This school," Steele said, addressing Long again, "would of course have to be funded. There would be materials. You'll need a new building, and money will have to be appropriated for teachers' salaries."

Long nodded. He and Steele had teamed up before on these contract deals, and they were both leaving much unsaid. The distance between here and Washington, and the general indifference toward Indians, made frontier fraud easy. The materials they would bill to the U. S. Government would be vastly different from whatever cheap trash was actually purchased for the benefit of the Cherokees. The government would be charged for a new school building when, in fact, both men knew they would simply use one of several abandoned buildings of cottonwood logs and mud already standing on the reservation. As for the monies that would be requested to pay teachers, Steele had ideas in that direction, too.

"Kristen!" he shouted, turning his head toward the stairwell behind him.

A young woman's voice answered hesitantly from above: "Yes, Pa?"

"C'mon down here for a minute."

Mankiller

Ephraim Long sat up straighter in his chair and combed his hair with his fingers. "And just how is your daughter doing, Hiram? She adjusting all right to the move from Wyoming?"

Steele shrugged one beefy shoulder. "Ah, you know how it is with women. Always moping and sulking. She's just like her ma was, God rest her soul. Kristen's only problem is too much time on her hands. She needs something useful to occupy her."

"Idle hands are the devil's playmates," Long said, a faint smile tugging at his lips. He was beginning to understand the drift things were taking, and he approved.

There were light footsteps on the stairs, a faint rustle of skirts and whiff of honeysuckle perfume. Then Kristen appeared in the doorway and paused there. She was a tall, slender girl of about 19 or 20 with almond-shaped eyes of bottomless blue and wheat-colored hair swept back under an amethyst comb. She made a point of avoiding Long's hawk-eyed stare, which she could almost feel probing her like greedy fingers.

Long stood up, followed by a slightly unsteady Red Jacket.

"Miss Steele." Long bowed low over the table. "And how are you this evening?"

"Fair to middling," she replied indifferently. Her father frowned at the cool tone.

"I wondered," Long said, his eyes still aggressively pursuing hers, "if you ever received the invitation I sent? The invitation to dine with me? Once each month I host a little soiree for some of our civic leaders. Your father has a standing invitation. But of course you're an adult now, and I thought you should receive your own invitation."

"My very own? It makes me feel like such a big girl."

Her sarcasm made Hiram double his fists in anger. He opened his mouth to speak, but Long beat him to it.

"I ask only because I never received your reply."

"Oh?" she said vaguely. "I could've sworn I posted it."

"Well?"

"Well what, Mr. Long?"

"Will you be attending?"

"I think not."

"May I ask why?"

Kristen's eyes ran from her father's. But she spoke up with surprising frankness. "Why? Because I don't enjoy eating fancy food purchased with money meant to feed starving Indians. While you and your civic leader friends stuff your faces at the soiree, I know of Cherokees who are hungry—especially since your bully policemen beat them up for the crime of hunting meat."

Her accusing stare met Red Jacket's surprised face. The chief flushed slightly and hastily pulled the cigar from his lips.

Steele had gotten his rage under control. He winked briefly at Long.

"Well now, daughter! All this here compassion you feel for the red man is downright noble. You sound just like those Quakers who write letters to *Harper's Magazine.* But are you ready to prove these noble feelings in someway besides sneaking around behind my back?"

Kristen's eyes narrowed in suspicion. She knew he was talking about the Cheyenne youth Touch the Sky, whom her father had driven off several years ago when he had caught Kristen and the boy meeting secretly. "What do you mean?"

"I mean that Chief Red Jacket and Ephraim here are looking to start a school on the reservation. How'd you like to be one of the teachers?"

For a moment Kristen's eyes had gone bright at this prospect. But the sly smirk on her father's face warned her.

"I'd love the chance, assuming there really will be a school. But I've noticed how things seem to get forgotten about around here once they're funded."

"Maybe you notice too much," Steele said, sudden anger spiking his tone. "Maybe you have too damn much time on your hands to worry about the goddamn pagan redskin—"

"Ah-hmm," Long said, casting a quick eye toward Chief Red Jacket.

Steele seemed to recollect himself. Then he changed his tack. A paternal smile eased onto his face.

"Well, Ephraim here is right, I suppose. Girl your age is a woman, especially out here. Either you'll take up a useful skill and make your living or you'll get married. Can't stay in the nest forever." The threat marking his tone was unmistakable.

"Marrying the right man out here," Long said, "could open up a whole new life. A man smart enough to avail himself of the ample opportunities. A man rich enough to give you the best things life has to offer."

"A man like you perhaps, Mr. Long?"

Long only smiled and flicked an ash off his duster. "Yes, Miss Steele. A man like me."

"If and when I do get married, Mr. Long, I hope it is to a man who makes a clear distinction between an opportunity and outright theft. There seem to be plenty of men"—here she glanced at her father, too—"who can't tell the difference. Now, if you gentlemen will excuse me, I'm rather tired and would like to rest."

By federal law it was illegal for white men to sell alcohol on Indian reservations. This did not prevent the proliferation of grog shops that infested the borders of the Indian Territory, bootlegging 40-rod whiskey to the Indians for their annuity blankets, flour, and pork.

Pawnee Creek formed the western border of the Great Bend Cherokee Reservation. It separated the reservation from the white settlement. Early in spring, swollen with snow melt and mountain runoff, the big creek was actually a small river.

Two Cherokees named Tassels and Dragging Canoe had slipped across the river after noon roll call on the reservation. They took several pairs of new beaded moccasins and an oilskin full of smoked fish with them. They visited the grog shop of a former mountain man named

Jediah Jones and swapped their goods for a few glasses of watered-down liquor. As the setting sun began to rim the western horizon in a copper glow, the two friends headed back toward their cabins on the reservation.

They had just swum Pawnee Creek, and were still climbing the grassy bank, when a sudden, sharp *whack* brought them up short. Both Indians recognized the dreaded sound: a boot being struck by a rawhide quirt. It was followed almost immediately by a voice as deep as a thunderclap.

"Why, see here! Two fish that got thrown up on the bank."

Tassels and Dragging Canoe stared up toward the crest of the bank. There stood Mankiller with one of his deputies on either flank. The sight half sobered both of them.

Again Mankiller whacked his boot with a quirt. He was a mountain of a man, thick limbed and barrel chested. Twin braids fell from under the distinctive broad-brimmed hat of the Cherokee tribal policemen: the hat turned up on the right side, the brim held to the crown by a small hook and eye. This allowed a rifle to be aimed from horseback even at a gallop.

His most striking feature, however, was his huge, powerful hands. Each finger was as thick as a picket pin, each knuckle like a big stone. They were powerful, menacing, dangerous hands—hands capable of choking a bull.

"These fish know the law," Mankiller said sadly to his deputies. "They know what happens to red men who get caught leaving the reservation."

"No," Tassels said, starting to back down toward the water. "No!"

But Mankiller's deputies moved with amazing skill and speed, leaping down the bank with ropes coiled in each hand. When the two lawbreakers started struggling too hard, Mankiller slid the Remington out of his sash and fired it once overhead. Now the two prisoners submitted quietly.

Casually Mankiller thumbed the spent cap out of the pistol and recharged the empty chamber. Below, his deputies trussed each victim similarly: both legs tied tight together at the ankles, left arm trussed tight to their sides. Only their right arms were left free.

"Toss them," Mankiller ordered.

One at a time, the deputies lifted the vigorously protesting men and carried them out into the swirling water, dropping them in. Desperately, heads bobbing up and down like corks, the one-armed swimmers struggled to make it back to shore. They choked and sputtered, sent up a wild, splashing spray. Quickly their breath began rasping in their chests.

Tassels made it to shore first.

"This fish is no good," Mankiller said. "Too small. Toss him back in."

Tassels barely had breath left to protest when the deputies picked him up and carried him out into the current. This scene was repeated several times with both men until they were limp with exhaustion. One of the deputies untied them and left them gasping in the grass.

Mankiller rode a big 16-hand bay. He returned

to his mount and squatted to untie the hobble. As always, he made a point of avoiding the right side, the Indian side, when he mounted, going around instead to the left side as white men did. He had just stepped up into the stirrup when the defiant words were shouted behind him.

"You are a bullying pig who licks the boots of white men!" Tassels said. "You and Red Jacket, two turncoats who help the white men destroy us! You have no honor, and I despise you."

Mankiller dropped his reins, slipped his feet from the stirrups and dismounted. Tassels had crawled to the top of the bank. He held a small rock in his right hand.

Mankiller grinned. "This fish is feisty! Perhaps I'll have to tie him back up, then ride to his cabin. He has a fine little wife waiting there for him. Perhaps I will lift her skirt and top her, show her what it's like with a real man."

Mankiller threw his head back and laughed. Tassels snarled in rage, staggered closer, and threw the rock.

It was a lucky toss and hit Mankiller square in the forehead, skewing his hat. But if he felt the fist-size rock hit him, he didn't show it— except that the mocking smile bled from his face, replaced by a gray, silent wrath.

Mankiller closed the distance between himself and Tassels, encircled the man's neck with his powerful hands. Mankiller's grip was so huge it cut off both the jugular and the trachea, stopping blood and air simultaneously. He squeezed one time, hard, and there was an audible snap like green wood breaking. Tassels tried to scream, but nothing came out except a gurgling froth of spittle.

Mankiller squeezed even harder, and Tassel's flailing feet left the ground. The Cherokee policemen held him up until he went slack, then threw his dead body to the ground and stared at Dragging Canoe.

"He attacked a Cherokee policeman. I killed him in self-defense. You got any complaint?"

Dragging Canoe, still too weak to rise from the grass, only stared at his dead companion. Tassels's neck had turned an ugly black and blue, swollen to twice its normal size.

Mankiller carefully straightened his hat. Then he returned to his horse, mounted, and rode out as if the dead man behind him was none of his business.

Chapter Three

"Brother," Little Horse said, "a thing troubles me." He and Touch the Sky had ridden out early, just as an old grandmother of the Crooked Lance Clan was singing the song to the new sun rising. Pockets of mist still floated over the Powder, and from the wooded thickets, orioles and thrushes sent up their warbling melodies.

Their legging sashes were stuffed with pemmican and dried plums, their foxskin quivers bristled with new arrows. Little Horse's four-barrel revolver protruded from the boot tied to his rope rigging; a percussion-action Sharps filled Touch the Sky's. Their ponies were battle rigged: lances, throwing axes, new oak bows—all were tied where they would be ready to hand if an attack came suddenly.

"Speak this thing which troubles you, buck."

"It is Wolf Who Hunts Smiling."

Touch the Sky frowned. "Truly, he is enough trouble for ten braves. But what of him?"

"He has always been mean and bloodthirsty. From the moment you were captured still wearing white man's clothing, Wolf Who Hunts Smiling has been eager to kill you. You have other dangerous enemies, the jealous Black Elk leading the pack. But, brother, Black Elk is at least loyal to his tribe. As you have learned the bitter way, Wolf Who Hunts Smiling not only lusts after power; he has no honor. Such men are dangerous. Now we are again riding out, what treachery will he stir up against you?"

Touch the Sky nodded. "You speak straight arrow, buck. He no longer has any honor, though once he did. He could have killed me after I pretended to summon a grizzly and saved him from the Pawnees. Instead, he lowered his rifle. And there was a time when he would not play the turncoat against his own tribe.

"But that time is smoke behind us. Now I know that he plotted with the Comanche Big Tree to kill our herd guards and steal our ponies. He has cleaned his parfleche of loyalty and stuffed it instead with ambition."

"And you," Little Horse said, "are blocking his path to glory. He knows he must either kill you or fail in his plans. I only hope this new trouble with our contract goods does not work in his favor. Many in the tribe are bitter and disappointed at being cheated, and he is clever at stoking their rage. And now he has this supposed shaman Medicine Flute to assist him in his treachery by claiming supernatural guidance. This further confuses the people."

Touch the Sky fell silent, letting his pony set her own pace across a loose shale slope. Caleb Riley's Far West Mining Company was a full sleep's ride from the Powder River camp. The mine itself was not located on Cheyenne hunting grounds, only the railroad spur line that hauled the ore to Laramie. Touch the Sky had served as pathfinder for the railroad crew, going up against the insane, murderous Sis-ki-dee—the Blackfoot renegade also known as the Contrary Warrior.

Recalling Sis-ki-dee's smallpox-scarred face, raggedly cropped short hair, and crazy-by-thunder eyes could still send a cold prickle down Touch the Sky's spine. But even more menacing were Arrow Keeper's recent words about this new trouble: *Be prepared to die before you are dead*. What could such apparent strong-mushroom talk possibly mean?

Sister Sun tracked higher across the hazy blue sky as the two young Cheyenne braves rode north toward the foothills of the Sans Arcs Mountains and Caleb Riley's mine. Although the Cheyenne tribe was currently at war with neither red men nor white, they kept a keen eye out for riders. Several times they paused to water their ponies in small streams and rills.

The battle will be hard, Arrow Keeper had warned him. *You will ride a great distance and find yourself in unfamiliar lands*. Arrow Keeper— his first and best friend in the tribe, a venerable old warrior and medicine man whose vision a long time ago at Medicine Lake had saved Touch the Sky's life. That vision foretold much suffering, but also much glory along Touch the Sky's turbulent path. Touch the Sky himself had finally experienced that same epic vision—and with that vision came his final determination to find his place once and for all as a Cheyenne.

Guiltily, Touch the Sky surfaced from these ruminations and woke to his surroundings. They were riding through a series of jagged cutbanks, the country rolling more now. They left the plains of the river bottom. How many times had he advised the young warriors to stop thinking so much and attend instead to the language of the senses? Fortunately, he could see that Little Horse was being vigilant for both of them.

For a moment Touch the Sky reached to feel the set of badger claws on the medicine pouch dangling from his clout. Arrow Keeper had given them to him, claiming it was the battle totem of Chief Running Antelope—Touch the Sky's dead father.

But there was no luxury now for such useless reflection. The trail suddenly narrowed and the two friends were forced to fall into single file. Touch the Sky tried to quell the activity of his thoughts, tried to observe things more with the hidden shaman's eye Arrow Keeper had taught him to open and see with.

Nonetheless, Arrow Keeper's warning from his latest medicine dream kept a claim on his awareness, nagging him like a sharp regret.

An old enemy from your past is back, and this time he means to kill you.

* * *

"It's got a damn bad smell to it," Caleb Riley said when Touch the Sky had finished speaking.

Caleb, Touch the Sky, Little Horse, and a burly man in twill coveralls named Liam McKinney stood around a wagon loaded with crushed rock. The two Cheyennes had made a simple meat camp in the foothills of the Sans Arcs the night before, riding in early the following day. Now morning sunlight illuminated the vast, dark scar of the mine, located farther up the mountainside above the mining camp.

"You sure," Liam said, "it wasn't just some stuff that got damaged or went bad during the hauling?"

Liam McKinney had a merry grin and plenty of laugh lines in a tough face. He had been the gang boss for the rail crew when the spur line was built. Caleb had kept him on to supervise the constant repair work to the rail line required by the rigorous mountain route, where spring melts, rock slides, and sabotage by Indians were common.

"Hell," Caleb said, answering for Touch the Sky, "hard slogging don't explain rocks in the bacon and blankets made of shoddy. It wasn't no damage, it was outright thievery."

Caleb was young and sported a shaggy blond beard. He was a big-framed man wearing buckskin trousers and shirt, with elkskin moccasins instead of boots. Nor was his preference for moccasins his only Indian trait. Touch the Sky recalled how impressed the Cheyenne tribe had been when they learned this white man hated

43

spurs and bridled his horse with a headstall only, refusing to shove a bit into its mouth.

"Any problem with last year's consignment?" Caleb said.

Touch the Sky shook his head. "Everything was delivered, and it was good quality."

"Well, the thing of it is," Caleb said slowly, puzzling it out, "we hired on a new business manager in Register Cliffs. Slick young feller, said he could start saving us money faster 'n a finger snap. One of the things he did, he put your supply contract up for bid. Told me he found a lower bidder to supply your tribe."

Caleb turned toward an unpainted clapboard office at the edge of the tent city formed by the campsite.

"I got the letter from him filed away someplace. Hold on a bit, I'll be right back."

While Caleb went to hunt for the letter, Touch the Sky translated the little he had learned so far for Little Horse, who spoke no English. All around them the camp came to life as miners emerged from their tents, yawning and scratching. They lined up outside the huge mess tent. Some stared curiously—some with open hostility—toward the new arrivals.

"Hey, shorty!" one of them called over to Little Horse. "That's a right purdy braid you got there. Maybe I'll cut it off for a soo-vee-neer!"

"You go ahead and try, pilgrim," Touch the Sky called back affably in English. "The white man's hell ain't half full."

The miner stared in surprise at the young buck's good English. But the lump of burn

44

tissue on Touch the Sky's chest, the network of bullet, arrow-point, and knife scars, the lean, tall, hard body, the grim and determined slit of his mouth—the miner took all this in and decided to take a sudden interest in staring at his own boots.

The door of the clapboard shack slapped open and Caleb stepped back outside, reading a letter.

"Here it is. Listen to this:"

"As for that other matter we discussed, I have good news. I have located a supplier in the Kansas Territory, the Frontier Supply Company, who has agreed to take on the contract to supply the Northern Cheyenne tribe located at the juncture of the Powder and Little Powder. This company has plenty of experience, being the sole supplier to the huge Cherokee reservation at Great Bend. They have assured me they will match the quality of the current supplier's goods while charging us one thousand dollars less."

Caleb looked up. "Tarnal hell! It's my fault. I never should've let him switch. They say you shouldn't pick up a happy baby. Your tribe was doin' fine with the last supplier."

"You didn't switch the goods," Touch the Sky assured his friend. "You've been plenty fair to us. Sounds to me like the source of the trouble is this Frontier Supply Company down in Great Bend. You got any names to go with it?"

Caleb scanned the letter. When he spoke the

familiar name, Touch the Sky felt cold blood rush into his face.

"Here you go. The man who signed the contract is named Steele. Hiram Steele."

An old enemy from your past is back, and this time he means to kill you.

Hiram Steele—hearing the name had opened a flood gate and sent memories tumbling through Touch the Sky's mind like storm-tossed driftwood. Memories of the quiet little copse where he used to meet Kristen Steele; memories of the ruthless hired hand, Boone Wilson, who had savagely beaten him at Steele's command; memories of his adopted parents' fear and suffering when Steele tried to drive them out of the mustang business, just as he had driven them out of the mercantile business.

Touch the Sky and Little Horse talked it over long and carefully during the ride back to camp. They agreed that a visit to the Great Bend Reservation was unavoidable. But they also agreed that, things being the way they were, it was best to try to avoid a regular council of the headmen. A routine council, with the tribe this angry over the shoddy goods, might be taken over by Touch the Sky's enemies.

The best plan, they agreed, was to ask old Arrow Keeper to take an extraordinary step. He must approach Chief Gray Thunder privately and ask him to secretly convene the Star Chamber.

The Star Chamber was the Cheyenne court of last resort. Made up of six headmen whose names were known only to Gray Thunder, the Star Chamber held extraordinary power and could override even votes of the Council of Forty. But because it was so powerful, any good Cheyenne chief was reluctant to abuse his authority by convening the Star Chamber.

Arrow Keeper listened carefully to his young apprentice. When Touch the Sky finished presenting his case, the old shaman nodded thoughtfully.

"I am loath to call on the Star Chamber. But I agree with you and Little Horse. This matter cannot go to council. Not now. Your enemies would hobble you. They would demand an attack on Caleb Riley and his miners.

"By indirection we will find our direction," he said quietly. "However, do not expect the Star Chamber to easily approve such a secret mission. I will do what I can. But if they say no, then it is hopeless."

While they waited to learn their fate, Touch the Sky and Little Horse went about their usual business. They mounted guard for the far-flung pony herds, drew camp sentry duty at night, and served as guards when the women and girls went out on the open plains to dig wild turnips, onions, and yarrow roots.

One day Touch the Sky rode into camp toward midday, having just been relieved on herd guard. He turned his pony loose in the rope corral. As he crossed to his tipi, he spotted the youth named Two Twists waiting near his entrance flap.

"Are you waiting for me, little brother?"

Two Twists assumed a look of exaggerated

innocence. "Waiting, Touch the Sky? Of course not. I was only strolling past. Only, now that you are here, I wonder a thing. Do you know a little pine-sheltered hollow just south of camp? Down the river a double stone's throw?"

Puzzled, Touch the Sky nodded. "I know it. What of it?"

Two Twists glanced across the clearing, toward the largest tipi in the Panther Clan circle.

"It is a very pleasant place to rest and meditate, is it not? And did you also know that Black Elk has ridden out on a scouting mission? That he will not return until sunset?"

With that, Two Twists suddenly added, "Well, I must go. I think I will walk over and talk to Honey Eater. Perhaps she might decide to take a walk."

Touch the Sky felt his blood suddenly humming when he realized what his loyal young friend was up to. As Two Twists started across the central clearing, Touch the Sky circled behind his tipi and angled down the long, sloping bank of the river. He stepped behind a willow brake and followed the current as it wound its way through hawthorn thickets and huge, narrow-leaved cottonwoods.

He reached the little sheltered place and slipped inside. The pines grew so thick they formed natural walls, and falling needles made a soft and springy bed underfoot. The wind gusted, soughing in the treetops with a rustling murmur.

Despite his usual warrior's vigilance, this quiet

place lulled him. He didn't hear Honey Eater approach. Suddenly, she was simply there beside him, her hand cool and light on the hard muscle of his shoulder.

"Is it really you this time?" she said, her voice a caress to his soul. "And not another dream tormenting me?"

She left her hand on his shoulder, dropped down to sit beside him. She had just braided her hair with petals of fresh white columbine, and the clean fragrance filled his nostrils. Touch the Sky buried his face in her hair, drew his lips to her nape, and delicately kissed the soft skin until he felt her shudder beneath him.

"If it is a dream," he murmured in reply, "I am having it, too."

For a long moment their eyes met and held, the shadow patterns on their faces changing as the pine boughs overhead swayed in the wind.

"You will soon be riding out again?" she said.

"Who told you this thing?"

"No one told me. No one had to. Lately the larks have quit singing. And I listened to the jays chatter about the great sadness to come."

Once again he was powerfully aware of not only her great beauty, but also her extraordinary perceptions and feelings. Honey Eater boasted of no shaman's skills. Yet long before the leaves turned their white sides up, Honey Eater knew a storm was coming.

"I may ride out," he said, "or I may not. I will know soon. But even if I go, the stone will still be there."

She leaned closer into him, both of them happy

with this rare intimacy. They both knew what stone he meant: the piece of marble he had placed on the ground in front of his tipi. That stone symbolized his love for her. Once, during vicious torture at the hands of the whiskey trader Henri Lagace, Touch the Sky had defied his tormentors by shouting out to Honey Eater, 'Do you know that I have placed a stone in front of my tipi? When that stone melts so, too, will my love for you.'

"I visit the stone when you are gone," she said. "Although sometimes doing so is dangerous."

She didn't need to elaborate. Black Elk had not found that stone yet, but he knew it was there and he had already punished her brutally for visiting it.

"You risk far too much to love me," he said.

"I would risk everything."

Those last words lingered in the air like a scent. Now each of them was thinking about the same thing: a promise Honey Eater had made when Touch the Sky rode out to fight the white buffalo hiders. Though the two of them had not performed the squaw-taking ceremony, in spirit they were already husband and wife. And Honey Eater had finally decided she would be his wife in body, too, whenever he sent for her. So far the great risk to her had held him back. But now they were alone.

He felt his heart stomping against his ribs and her breath moist and warm on his eyelids. Their eyes met again, his bright with powerful desire, hers turning to liquid under the burn of his stare.

One rawhide string held Honey Eater's soft doeskin dress closed in front. Without willing it, Touch the Sky raised one hand and untied the thong. The soft flaps fell back, revealing the high and hard swells of her breasts. A soft moan of surrender escaped her lips as he lowered his mouth over one plum-colored nipple and gently kissed it stiff.

Fire blazed to life in his loins, and the need was on him to merge his flesh with this woman he loved. He pressed her back into the soft mat of pine needles, feeling her body yield and mold to his.

Abruptly, so close they both started, an owl hooted. Only they both knew it was no owl. Two Twists was warning them that danger approached!

Quickly, his breathing still clumsy with desire, Touch the Sky closed Honey Eater's dress. Then he rose and slid through the shifting shadows to the edge of the hollow. Cautiously he peered out, glanced both ways along the river bank. Then he saw several old grandmothers approaching from camp, reed baskets over their arms as they gathered rushes for weaving.

His disappointment was keen. They might soon wander into the hollow. He could not endanger Honey Eater any longer. He slipped back and said low in her ear, "Somebody is coming. You stay here as if you were merely resting and enjoying the quiet. Good-bye, sweet Honey Eater. Think of me."

"How will I think of anything else?"

Already he was stealing toward the opposite

side of the pine hollow, planning to double around back into camp.

"Touch the Sky?" she said and he turned around. "Be careful, and come back to me." She crossed her wrists over her heart: Cheyenne sign-talk for love.

He crossed his, too, then slipped out of the thicket. He returned to camp, unobserved, and lifted the entrance flap of his tipi.

His breath caught in his throat: a figure was standing there in the grainy shadows of the interior.

"The Star Chamber has met," Arrow Keeper said. "You and Little Horse will ride to the Cherokee reservation to defeat this hair-face thief called Hiram Steele."

Chapter Four

For this mission, saving time was not as crucial as conserving strength. Therefore, Touch the Sky and Little Horse did not push their ponies hard on the ride south and east toward Great Bend. Remounts would be too cumbersome, yet neither brave was eager to show up riding exhausted ponies among potential enemies in a strange land. And more than one man without remounts had died after his only horse foundered on the plains.

Instead, they let their spirited ponies set their own pace, grazing them often in the lush buffalo grass and resting them frequently. Nor did the two braves neglect to build their own strength. Game was plentiful as they moved onto new ranges. They spotted plenty of elk and antelope, prairie chickens and rabbits, even a small herd of buffalo. Tribal sanction would not permit the killing of buffalo except during the annual buffalo hunt. But everything else was fair game, and the two youths made every camp a meat camp. The river growth supplied blackberries, elderberries, and chokecherries.

In fact, the long journey was so easy that Touch the Sky sometimes had to remind himself they were riding into great danger. Mostly the terrain was typical plains country, flat or gently rolling, wooded bluffs and tableland near the rivers and major streams. Lush new grass grew knee high and often they rode through vast meadows of gaily blooming flowers: white columbine, blue morning glories, and yellow buttercups.

Despite such natural beauty and bounty, the image of Hiram Steele's cold, flint-gray eyes seldom deserted Touch the Sky. And a work crew stringing the white men's talking wire, or the occasional patrol of blue-bloused pony soldiers, kept him and Little Horse carefully scanning the horizons.

Nor was nature always friendly. Several times they were caught out in the open under sudden downpours that almost instantly turned the ground to mud. Other times, violent windstorms kicked up out of nowhere, threatening to choke them in thick, debris-strewn dust.

Caleb had sat down with Touch the Sky and carefully traced the location of Great Bend on a good army map. The two Cheyennes knew the town itself—which they must carefully avoid, especially since they would be considered renegades far from their legal homeland—was located on a wooded bluff beside Pawnee Creek. This big creek, actually a small river at this time of year, was also the western border of the Cherokee reservation.

Finally, weary but wary, the two Cheyennes crested a long slope and spotted a bluff rising in the distance. The high false fronts of a few frame buildings and a lone white church steeple rose up against the gray sky.

"Great Bend," Touch the Sky said. "It must be. We cannot see Pawnee Creek from here, but all that land beyond is the Cherokee nation."

"From where I sit now, brother," Little Horse said, "it looks like most of the land hair faces give to the red man. Empty and useless, good neither for hunting or the gardens that palefaces are so keen to see us hoe with the women."

Touch the Sky nodded. "We get the land they do not want. Until they discover the yellow rocks on it. Then it is time to get a chief drunk on strong water so the red men can be moved farther west. These Cherokees have been driven even farther from their ancient lands than our tribe was."

Having little contact with them, the two Cheyenne braves knew only a little about this proud tribe from east of the river called Great Waters. They had been hunters and farmers back east, and though they had taken on many of the white man's ways, they had also fought some fierce battles against them and were said to be no warriors to fool with. Touch the Sky hoped that warrior tradition still lived in these people. If

Arrow Keeper's vision was true, a hard fight lay ahead.

"We will skirt the town by riding through the trees behind the bluff," Touch the Sky said, pointing. "Then we will ford Pawnee Creek and ride onto the reservation. First we must search for a good, safe camp."

Little Horse nodded. His eyes met his friend's. The sturdy little brave grinned.

"Brother, we are up against it again! I fought Hiram Steele beside you in Bighorn Falls when we saved your white clan's ranch. We beat him then, buck! What Cheyennes have done, Cheyennes will do."

But as they pointed their buffalo-hair bridles north toward the shelter of the trees, Touch the Sky admitted to himself that he felt far less confident than his friend's bold words. They had not one ally in this entire land, yet no doubt more than enough enemies. If whites spotted them, most likely they'd be shot on sight. Nor did he know if the Cherokees would be any less hostile toward Cheyenne interlopers.

Besides, he had learned to pay attention to the newly awakened sixth sense that Arrow Keeper had taught him to use. And that sixth sense told him bad trouble was extremely close at hand.

The two young Cheyenne warriors angled north and rode single file through a forest of sycamore and oak, dense with deadfalls and undergrowth. They emerged on the bank of what must be Pawnee Creek, well upstream from the settlement of Great Bend.

The water flowed near to the top of the banks, the current churning foam where trapped branches had formed a sawyer out in midstream. But the bottom was solid and the well-rested ponies waded in gamely, swimming the rest of the way with little difficulty. They climbed out on the opposite bank and set first foot on the Cherokee reservation.

"Brother," Little Horse said, "things do not look any better from here. Look there, how the grass has already been overgrazed. See how barren this land is of trees except here by the water. I am no farmer as these Cherokees are said to be. But I have been told that farmers like to plant their crops in soil good enough to support trees, especially nut trees for these grow where the best soil is."

Touch the Sky nodded, looking carefully all about them. His uneasy feeling had increased despite the apparent emptiness.

"Speaking of trees, before we ride farther let us climb one and see what we can see."

The sun blazed behind them, casting elongated shadows to the east. They shinnied up the bole of a huge cottonwood tree. From its uppermost branches they got a good view of the new Cherokee homeland, and it was discouraging to their plans.

Getting about unobserved would be a nearly impossible task. Most of the visible land was barren or given over to cultivation or the grazing of livestock. Small herds of sheep and cows were clumped here and there, alternating with small fields or kitchen gardens surrounded by fences.

Tidy cabins of cottonwood logs chinked with mud were scattered here and there. They spotted a figure with twin braids protruding from under a floppy-brimmed hat, moving patiently up and down behind a mule and harrow.

"Buck," Little Horse called over from a nearby limb, "it is going to be the Wendigo's own work, moving about without being spotted. There is no cover! Where will we make a camp?"

"Straight words, *Shaiyena*. As for moving about, we must operate as we did when we fought Hiram Steele's men before."

"You mean, move about by night?"

Touch the Sky nodded. Cheyennes did not normally like to leave the safety of their firepits after dark. But he and Little Horse had learned to make a virtue of necessity.

"As for a camp," Touch the Sky said, "clearly our only hope is Pawnee Creek. We must find a secluded spot from which to operate. And where else could we water our ponies safely? I think we should ride north, farther from town."

Little Horse approved this plan. Just before he climbed down, Touch the Sky felt another uneasy prickling at his nape. Again he glanced carefully around them, spotting nothing to cause alarm.

They slipped the hobbles off their ponies' fore-legs and bore slowly north again, watching for opportune spots. Several times they encountered a promising copse or hollow. But when Touch the Sky searched for signs of animals, he found few. This hinted that men had recently passed through these areas, so they rode on.

Sister Sun was now a dull orange ball just above the horizon. Still they had found no spot safe enough to trust. Worse yet, the trees and ground cover began to thin out as they moved farther north. Discouraged, they turned their ponies and retraced their steps.

It was too quiet. They heard only the steady rhythm of cicadas and the harsh calls of grebes and red-tailed hawks circling overhead.

They were forced to pass dangerously close to the white settlement. Only a cypress brake and dense thickets protected them. They heard occasional noises from town: the rattling of trace chains, a shout of greeting. Both Cheyennes rode quietly, letting their ponies walk. They watched for any sign of danger: birds suddenly taking off from the bank or their ponies abruptly pricking their ears forward.

The sun still shone, but the shadows were deepening. They reached a dog-leg bend in the river. Touch the Sky bent low to avoid an over-hanging branch; when he sat back up again, fear suddenly stuck a lance point in him.

A giant bear of an Indian sat his saddle directly ahead of him—a huge Cherokee with a broad-brimmed hat turned up on the right side. A Spencer carbine was balanced across his saddletree.

"Fly like the wind, brother!" he said to his friend, suddenly pulling hard on his hackamore and turning his calico mustang around.

But now Touch the Sky saw they had ridden into a death trap. Four more heavily armed

Cherokees sat their mounts across the trail behind them! They wore butternut-colored hats exactly like the other one's.

The creek flowed by to their left, but they would be shot before they reached the halfway point. Beyond it a fairly steep bank gave way to the settlement—hardly good cover. They were trapped despite their combined vigilance. Whoever these Cherokees were, they were no novices at silent movement.

"Brother," Little Horse said quietly, "do we draw and fight?"

"Perhaps we will have to," Touch the Sky said grimly. "But hold off a moment."

He reined his pony back around to face the lone figure ahead, clearly the leader. He knew many Cherokees spoke good English. So he spoke in that language.

"We have come in peace. We are Northern Cheyennes from the Powder River country. We have no quarrel with our Cherokee brothers."

The big Cherokee's face registered momentary surprise at the stranger's good command of English. He replied in a voice so deep it seemed to vibrate Touch the Sky's skin.

"Brothers? Did you suck my mother's dug? Oh, but we have a quarrel, Cheyenne. You say you come in peace. But only look at your pony's rigging! That is a battle rig or I will eat my hat. By what right do you sneak onto our land ready for battle?"

"Ready for battle is not a battle," Touch the Sky said. "On the frontier, only a fool would not be ready."

He knew this was another kind of trap. For Touch the Sky and Little Horse could have no way of knowing who these Cherokees were, whether they served white masters like Hiram Steele or their own people. It was not yet safe to state the true purpose of this visit.

"You speak of owning the land, like the whiteskins do," Touch the Sky bluffed. "We know nothing of any Indian land. We are merely trying to skirt the white settlement. We are traveling south to visit our Southern Cheyenne kin."

The big Cherokee seemed to consider this reply. After all, it was quite possible. There were indeed Cheyennes camped to the south of this place. But Mankiller really didn't care who they were or what their purpose was in being here. It was all one to him—the main thing was to have a little fun.

Touch the Sky watched the big Cherokee whack his boot with his quirt. Even from this distance, Touch the Sky easily saw the big hands, each finger like a thick rope.

"I am called Mankiller," the Cherokee said. "I am Chief of the Cherokee Tribal Police. But our justice is not bound by the white man's law-ways. I am the sheriff, the judge, and the jury. And I find both of you guilty."

"Guilty of what?"

"Guilty of trespassing with the intention of committing some mischief."

"Trespassing! That is white man's peyote talk. How can Indians trespass? We are only passing by."

"Good," Mankiller said. He signaled to his men. "After such a long ride, perhaps it is time for a cool swim."

Little Horse looked at Touch the Sky, waiting for the signal. But Touch the Sky shook his head. Only if they were clearly about to be killed would he signal for resistance against such odds. These braves had the cold, flat gaze of experienced killers.

One at a time, they were each dragged roughly from their ponies. The weapons trained on them made resistance useless. Mankiller's deputies bound their legs tightly together with rawhide cords and strapped one arm to their side, leaving just one free. Touch the Sky understood why when two of the deputies hoisted him like a sack of grain and splashed into the water with him.

He felt himself being swung, heaved. Then he hit the ice-cold water. Unable to kick, he swam desperately with one arm, barely keeping his chin out of the water. Another splash nearby told him Little Horse, too, had been thrown in.

"Look at the odd fishes!" a Cherokee warrior taunted. "Are they trout with braids?"

"No, they are Cheyenne warrior fish!"

"They swam all the way down from the north country just to call us their brothers!"

"They have no quarrel with us. They only want to swim and play."

Touch the Sky neared the bank slowly, but it was impossible to swim straight with only one arm. He was immediately seized and thrown back out into midstream. Little Horse received similar treatment.

Already Touch the Sky's swimming arm was exhausted from the hard, constant motion of staying above surface in the brisk-moving current. Once, twice, again he went under, water rushing down his throat and choking him. He made it close to shore once again, coughing and gasping, and again he was flung back.

Over and over he and Little Horse made it close to shore only to be tossed back in. Now his arm was so weak it felt heavy as a stone club, and he was swallowing more and more water. The merciless taunts continued although by now he heard little in his desperate struggle to stay alive.

Another mouthful of water choked him until he almost blacked out. He went under and barely managed to break surface. Again he reached shore, so exhausted his heart was stomping his ribs and his breathing came in short, ragged gasps. And now Touch the Sky finally realized he was only a few heartbeats away from death.

His foot struck bottom. Hands grasped him, ready to heave him out one more time. Only this time, he knew, would be the last. He could swim no more. Clearly Little Horse, too, was utterly exhausted.

As Touch the Sky was lifted and swung, he began chanting his death song. But before his captors could heave him to his death, a high-pitched scream rose from the bank above them—a young woman's scream.

"Stop it!" the new arrival demanded. "Oh, please dear God, stop it!"

The expected toss never came. His head hanging upside down, water running out of his lungs, Touch the Sky looked up toward the top of the bank.

It took him a long moment to understand what he was seeing. The tall, pretty, horrified blonde standing with one fist squeezed to her mouth in fright was his first love, Kristen Steele!

Chapter Five

There was a long, surprised silence after Kristen's outburst. All the Indians, including the half-drowned Cheyennes, stared at the pretty girl. Her sunbonnet was tilted back to reveal an oval face with skin as fair and flawless as moonstone. The modest blue cotton dress could not completely hide full, high breasts and the long sweep of her hips. Her presence near the creek was explained by the wicker basket hooked over her left arm, bright with golden daffodils and scarlet verbena.

Mankiller's sudden laugh broke the stillness. It was loud as a clap of thunder.

"What? The daughter of Hiram Steele begging for Indians? I could understand this pity if we were kicking a dog. Everyone knows that paleface girls like to hug and kiss pups. But does the little sun-haired one know that these Cheyennes eat dogs? Indeed, I hear they boil their favorite puppies until they float in the pot. Then, their eyes streaming tears, they praise the animals' virtues while chewing their eyeballs."

Kristen, realizing the danger to Touch the Sky and Little Horse, had quickly hidden her shock at recognizing them.

"I suppose that's why you're drowning them? Because the Cheyenne people eat dogs?" she said indignantly.

Mankiller threw back his head and laughed again, whacking his boot with his quirt.

"Stomp your foot, Sun Hair," he teased her. "Then you look like a fiery little warrior!"

Kristen looked as if she did indeed want to stomp her foot. Instead, she only said coldly, "I thought you were supposed to be a lawman, not a bully. These two have done nothing."

Something in her tone made Mankiller suspicious. He lost his mocking smile, staring hard at her.

"You are quick to champion strangers. And how are you so sure they have done nothing? Any man is guilty if you ask him the right question. Or do you perhaps know them well enough to bespeak their honesty?"

"Of course not. But whatever they might've done," she said hastily, "surely they don't deserve to die?"

"Die? But Golden Top, I am not killing them.

Only bathing the trail dust off our Cheyenne guests. A bit of fun."

Kristen frowned. "Yes. A bit of fun like you had with Tassels."

The amused glint left Mankiller's eyes. "Already the whites have heard about Tassels? It is an Indian matter. He attacked me."

Clearly Kristen had more she wanted to say on that score. But she bit back any reply. Instead, she only said, "Will you let these two go now?"

Touch the Sky and Little Horse were sprawled on the grassy bank, sides still heaving. Mankiller stared at them. "The sun-haired girl with her nose in the air amuses me. I like her haughty manner. You two drowned rats may go. But witnesses hear me when I say I am ordering you off the Cherokee reservation permanently. If I or any of my men see you here again, we will kill you. Do you understand?"

Both Cheyennes had sat up by now. Touch the Sky nodded once.

"Good," Mankiller told them. "Now ride. You may follow the creek until out of sight of the town. But keep riding, and you must avoid the reservation."

Touch the Sky rose unsteadily, his body exhausted from the ordeal. He joined Little Horse in a hard struggle up the bank. The Cherokees had not touched their weapons or gear. But all five policemen held rifles and pistols on them, making sure they didn't make any sudden moves.

They swung onto their ponies, chucked them up the bank. Kristen had turned as if to return to town. With her back to the Cherokees below, she said in a voice meant just for Touch the Sky:

"Sneak into town after dark, but be careful! I live in the white two-story house at the end of Congress Street. Watch for a light in the back upstairs window—that's my room."

She dared say no more, but Touch the Sky heard her. Holding his face impassive, revealing nothing, he pointed his bridle downstream and rode south of Great Bend, the Cherokee policemen silently watching until the two Cheyennes disappeared in the thickets.

A policeman named Creek Hater looked at Mankiller. "Those two mean trouble. We will see them again."

Mankiller nodded. A little grin twitched at his lips.

"I know we will. That is why I let them go, not for her. I am curious about their purpose in coming here. We will kill them, all in good time. But first let us enjoy a little sport with them."

At first the two friends did as instructed. They stuck close to Pawnee Creek until the settlement of Great Bend was out of sight. But as soon as it was dark, Touch the Sky halted them. He had already explained the brief message from Kristen, whom Little Horse had recognized immediately as the beauty from Bighorn Falls.

"Uncle Moon is hiding among the clouds tonight," Touch the Sky said. "We should ride back to Great Bend now while light is scarce."

Little Horse agreed. "When we get close, we

can tether our ponies back at the creek and sneak in on foot."

"The town will be dark. Still, we will be up against it if we are spotted sneaking about at night. We will be shot on sight."

"Nor can we be sure," Little Horse said, "where this stone-faced Mankiller is lurking. Brother, I looked deep into the crazy eyes of the Blackfoot named Sis-ki-dee. And I glimpsed the mad light in the eyes of Big Tree, the Comanche Terror. But this Cherokee is colder than either of them.

"I say it now, and this place hears me. Of all the dangers we will face on this mission, he will surely be the worst. His eyes tell me he lives up to his name, and I fear he takes great pleasure in what he does best."

They turned their ponies and made good time despite the dark night. The water whispered and chuckled to their right; occasionally a lone coyote raised a solitary howl from the vast plains to their left. They chewed on pemmican and dried plums, feeling the air grow cooler and cooler against their bare skin.

Touch the Sky was even more silent than usual. Seeing Kristen Steele so suddenly had jarred him to the core of his soul. Old feelings that he had thought were long dead surfaced from the burial ground of painful memories. Feelings which troubled and confused him—especially with the recent touch of Honey Eater's tender flesh still burning his skin.

Soon the lights of Great Bend winked into view. They found a good patch of graze near the water and tethered their ponies with long strips of rawhide. After a brief debate, they decided to take no weapons except their knives. Despite the moonless night, they took the precaution of smearing their bodies and faces with mud from the creek. Knowing some dogs would be on guard, they determined the wind direction so they could approach into it.

Great Bend fit the pattern of many settlements on the American frontier. A tightly grouped cluster of houses and businesses was bisected once by a main central street and crossed in the opposite direction by several side streets. There was no gradual change from town to surroundings. The buildings simply stopped and the prairie grass took over.

This practical layout made the settlement easy to approach. The two Cheyennes took advantage of hillocks and swales, moving within a stone's throw of the nearest building.

"Wait here a little," Touch the Sky whispered. "I can read the signs that name the streets. Once I find Congress Street, I will come back for you. I do not like the thought of us sneaking around inside their town until we know exactly where to go."

This made sense and Little Horse nodded. Touch the Sky listened for a long time before he moved out. He could hear piano notes tinkling from a saloon, and it surprised him that he easily recognized the tune from his days among the whites: "Little Brown Jug." Now and then a voice called out or a horse whickered. Otherwise, all seemed quiet.

The Cheyenne rose, sprinted to the back of the building, and hugged the frame wall as he followed the shadows around to the street it faced on. A quick glance both ways told Touch the Sky that all the buildings on this street were businesses. He stayed in the apron of shadows and moved to the first side street. Luck was with him. A crudely painted shingle nailed to a corner building identified this collection of deep wagon ruts as Congress Street.

Touch the Sky ducked back just in time—a trio of riders came down the main street, hoofclops echoing off the high false fronts. They passed an open doorway, and the light within washed over them. They were wranglers, judging from their sharp-roweled spurs, woolly chaps, and bright bandannas.

The Cheyenne glanced both ways down Congress Street and spotted one two-story house. It sat all the way at the far end of the street, surrounded by a big yard but no fence. Touch the Sky made a quick map in his mind, then sneaked back to get Little Horse.

Touch the Sky leading, the two braves avoided the streets altogether. They moved in a wide berth around the town, approaching from the open vastness to the rear of the Steele residence.

Even as they crept near, a lantern flared to life in the upstairs window. A pale, slanting shaft of light stabbed down into the backyard like a bony finger. Touch the Sky saw Kristen's figure move into the window, searching the darkness below.

"Wait there," he said to Little Horse, pointing to a little storage shed behind the house. "If I am spotted I will run like a thieving coyote, and you had best do the same. This is no place to get caught in a fight. If we must flee, we will meet back at the ponies."

Little Horse nodded. Touch the Sky glided forward, silent as a shadow. When he was close to the house he groped for a pebble and flung it up against the window.

He heard it open. Then Kristen whispered, "Is that you, Matthew?"

His old name struck his ear with an odd, unfamiliar sound. "It's me," he whispered back.

"If you're careful, I think you can climb up the lightning rod. But do be careful please! My pa is downstairs in his study, and he's got ears like a cat."

Touch the Sky's moccasins made little noise, yet gripped well, as he clung to the metal pole and walked his way up the side of the house.

Just shy of the window casement, a shingle broke under Touch the Sky's foot. The board cracked loudly and clattered against the house as it fell. To make matters worse, Touch the Sky lost his footing and banged one knee loudly against the house.

"Kristen!" Steele's voice shouted from downstairs. "What the hell you doing up there?"

Kristen turned white as new snow and whirled from the window. "Nothing, Pa! I just dropped something."

His heart pounding in his throat, Touch the Sky finished his hazardous climb. Moments later he stood beside Kristen in a small but tidy room. A bed with an eiderdown quilt, an oak highboy, a washstand, an armoire on clawed feet, and a single ladderback chair made up the room's furnishings. Some of the flowers Kristen had gathered earlier had been placed in a pottery vase atop the highboy.

They stepped back away from the window. The lantern's light revealed a wild and magnificent spectacle to the girl's eyes. Clearly the half-naked man standing before her, his body smeared with musty-smelling mud, was a savage. His hair hung in a confusion of tangled black locks, and some of his many scars were visible even through the layer of mud. And the stains on the beaded sheath of his knife—surely they were old bloodstains! And yet, his piercing black eyes were bright with intelligence. His high cheeks and hawk nose lent his face a handsome nobility and strength.

"Is it really you, Matthew?" she said. "Are you really standing here next to me?"

Arrow Keeper had buried Touch the Sky's white name forever. But now it sounded right again on her lips, as if the intervening years had suddenly been erased.

"It's really me, right enough. But I wouldn't be standing here if you hadn't saved my bacon earlier. I thank you, lady."

"Matthew, I'm so happy to see you I could just burst! But what are you doing here? Don't you understand? My father hates you with a passion that frightens me. He's the brooding type. And he's been brooding ever since you and Little

Horse whipped him at Bighorn Falls. If he finds out you're here, he'll move heaven and earth to kill you."

"He'll find out soon enough. Your father is why I'm here."

Briefly, he explained about the load of bogus contract goods delivered to the Cheyennes—worthless goods traced back to Hiram Steele's Frontier Supply Company.

Kristen's eyes blazed with anger by the time Touch the Sky finished speaking. "I've heard my father boasting about how much profit he made from a delivery to the Northern Cheyennes. Knowing him, I suspected shady dealings. But I never dreamed it was your tribe."

"The loss of the goods is bad enough. My people need those things and looked forward to them all winter. But I'm the one who talked the tribe into trusting Caleb Riley in the first place. It leaves both of us smelling mighty bad to the tribe."

"Oh, Matthew, it's awful! I hate my father. If I had money of my own, somewhere to go, I'd be long gone by now. I've even considered—well, considered a loveless marriage just to get away from him. But, Matthew, what can you possibly do?"

"My tribe is powerless to fight your father in the courts. No jury in the country would convict a white man for fraud against Indians who haven't signed a recent government treaty. But the Cherokees can fight him because he's robbing them, too."

"Of course he is," she said bitterly. "But you

can't fight him, Matthew, he—"

"I whipped him before and I'll do it again."

"Matthew, no! Don't you see? You met Mankiller and his police today. Who do you think pays their wages? My father."

"I didn't ride all this way to talk it over."

"That's it? You're determined to fight?"

He nodded.

"Nothing will change your mind?"

"Nothing."

She studied his face closely, debating something. Then, abruptly, she turned and crossed to the highboy. She took a folded sheet of paper from the top drawer.

"Well, if you're mule mind is made up," she said, "take this. It's a letter my father wrote to Ephraim Long. He's the agent for the Great Bend Reservation. I found it recently. You can see where father spilled ink on it, which is why he never sent it. Probably wrote it over—he's obsessed with neatness. I don't know what you can do with it, if anything."

Touch the Sky unfolded the note and read it quickly.

"It might come in handy," he said, folding the note again and tucking it carefully into his parfleche. "I'm surprised he put this in writing. Maybe he thought better of it and never sent it. Anyway, thanks. Now I need one more favor from you—not that you haven't done enough already."

"What"

"A name. The name of one good Cherokee brave who might be willing to fight what your father and Mankiller are doing."

She shook her head. "It's too dangerous. Nobody—"

"Listen, lady. There's always somebody willing to fight. Always one person willing to stand up if he gets half the chance. Just give me one name."

"Well, there is someone who I've heard my father and Long call a troublemaker. One who doesn't like Chief Red Jacket. His name is Jack Morningstar. He's a skilled tradesman, a cooper. He makes barrels and kegs for my father's company. My father employs him because he does good work cheap. But believe me, there's no love lost between them."

"How would I find him?"

"His cabin is located at a place called Sundown Ridge, not far from where you had your run-in with Mankiller. Just due east from there. Two rain barrels out front."

"Good."

A thump from downstairs made Kristen start.

"I had better go," Touch the Sky said. "Little Horse is waiting."

"Matthew?"

"Hmm?"

Suddenly they were both aware of how close together they were standing. Her honeysuckle perfume teased his nostrils, and he watched a vein pulse in her soft white throat.

"Do you remember when my father ordered Boone Wilson to beat you up?"

"How could I forget?"

"Well, do you also remember when you asked

me—in front of my father and Wilson—if I wanted to see you again?"

His pained silence was answer enough.

"Matthew, I lied when I said no. Don't you see? I was so scared for you. I was afraid that if I told the truth it would get you killed right there."

Despite all the years and battles and suffering since then, a huge weight of doubt was lifted from his chest. A smile divided his face.

"Then it's prob'ly a good thing you lied. That lie helped send me packing. And they would have killed me if I had stayed."

"And they'll kill you now if you aren't careful."

Another noise came from downstairs, as if to emphasize Kristen's warning. For a moment she stepped up on her toes to kiss him lightly. "If you're determined to fight, I'm going to do what I can to help you. There's a shed in the backyard. Some bricks are piled by the door. If I have a message for you, I'll put it under the bricks."

He nodded. "Thanks. I mean it. But don't cross your pa."

She turned down the wick and he wriggled back out the window. He was halfway down the lightning rod when he heard her whisper his name into the darkness.

"Matthew? Don't you cross him either. Please be careful!"

Chapter Six

Touch the Sky and Little Horse knew it was useless to search for a campsite that night. So once again they followed Pawnee Creek south at a good pace, leaving Great Bend well behind.

They found a spot sheltered by willows and made a simple cold camp for the rest of the night. They put down a canvas groundsheet Little Horse had won from a Lakota in a pony race, then unrolled their buffalo robes. After watering their ponies and picketing them in good graze, they stretched out under a star-shot sky. Touch the Sky reported his conversation with Kristen.

"The girl with sunlight trapped in her hair," Little Horse said when his friend had finished. "The girl you once held in your blanket for love talk. And now you have climbed into her lodge—and perhaps will again?"

"Why do you play the coy maiden, buck? Speak straight arrow and tell me the thing you mean."

"I mean only that she is very beautiful. That when she looks at you, the sun shines in her eyes, too. You must be careful. I have seen how you look at her."

Little Horse stopped there. He was too good of a friend to embarrass Touch the Sky by saying Honey Eater's name. But Little Horse had a deep affection for her, as did most in the tribe. He trusted his friend, yet his brotherly concern for Honey Eater made him protective; and after all, this pretty golden-haired girl was a paleface. If she lured Touch the Sky back into her world, Little Horse would lose a blood brother.

The next day they began searching early for good shelter. At one point, skirting a thick deadfall of brambles, Touch the Sky felt his shaman sense tingle at the back of his neck. He took a closer look at the seemingly impenetrable deadfall. A tunnel had been burrowed through it, the result, perhaps, of large animals.

He bade little Horse wait while he explored the tunnel. After a few feet, the tunnel opened up into a clear corridor that permitted him to stand. Enough light filtered through to show him the dark cave entrance ahead, leading back under the steep bank.

He poked his head in carefully. But if any wild animals had sheltered here, they were long gone. There was no animal smell lingering. The cave formed a dry shelter about the size of a tipi. He returned to Little Horse and explained his find.

"Look," his friend said, walking well to one side of the deadfall. He pointed toward an opening in the trees. It was hard to spot at a quick glance. "We can tether our ponies there by day and graze them out away from the creek after dark. It will be risky, but this is a fool's mission anyway—the only kind we seem to favor."

They stored their gear in the cave, dug a firepit, and moved the ponies into the hidden clearing. Little Horse killed a fat rabbit, then spitted it with the same arrow that had killed it. They cooked it over the firepit, then enjoyed their first hot meal in two sleeps.

"What next, brother?" Little Horse said, licking grease from his fingers.

"We can do nothing by ourselves. This is not just a Cheyenne battle, but a Cherokee battle, too. We have to help these red men find their fighting fettle."

"How?"

"Jack Morningstar," Touch the Sky said. "He is our only chance. After dark, we will pay him a visit."

The two Cheyennes took turns sleeping for the rest of that day, one remaining on guard outside the hidden cave. After dark they rigged their well-rested ponies. Then, fording the creek, they entered the Cherokee reservation.

A full moon and a starry sky made night riding easy, but also exposed them. They moved by carefully predetermined bounds, always picking an object dead ahead to aim for so they would not wander astray. They avoided ridges that might give them away, sticking to the swales and ground cover.

Once in a while one of them would dismount and place his fingers lightly to the ground, feeling for the vibrations of riders. Even so, they made good time. Soon they had reached the long, narrow spine that Touch the Sky guessed must have been Sunset Ridge.

Moonlight backlit the ridge, limning a small cabin with a light blazing in one oil-paper-covered window.

"Two rain barrels out front," Touch the Sky said, pointing. "Jack Morningstar."

They hobbled their ponies foreleg to rear. Then they climbed the rest of the way up the ridge. Several barrels and kegs, in various stages of completion, littered the cooper's yard. Nearby was a pond fed by a quiet rill. They stopped well back from the dwelling.

"Hello, the cabin!" Touch the Sky called out in English. "Is this Jack Morningstar's place?"

After a long silence, punctuated by the throaty croaking of bullfrogs near the pond, a man said suspiciously, "I don't recognize your voice. Step into the light."

The two Cheyennes did as instructed.

"What the hell? You Sioux?"

"Cheyenne."

"I'll be—"

A squat, solid man wearing machine-made trousers and a flannel shirt stepped into the doorway. He wore his hair in long twin braids.

He held an ax loosely in his left hand.

"An English-speaking Cheyenne who knows my name. Should I be scared or curious?"

"I'll explain everything," Touch the Sky said. "But can we step out of this light first? The last thing we need is to be spotted by Mankiller again."

A sympathetic look passed over Morningstar's deadpan face. He set the ax aside. "So you've met the noble lawman of the reservation. Well, stranger, any enemy of Mankiller's is welcome here. Come in."

The inside of the one-room cabin was as spartan as the exterior: a shakedown bed in the back corner, a rammed-earth floor, a crude deal table with kegs scattered about for seats. Crossed sticks on the back wall formed shelves for a few pottery dishes.

Little Horse stared at the coal-oil lantern, marveling that such a small flame could give off so much light—and how could this cloudy water inside it actually burn like wood?

Morningstar looked at their clouts, the tufts of enemy scalps tied to their sashes, the hunted-animal gleam in their eyes.

"You two ain't no praying Indians," he said with conviction. "You lost or just drunk?"

Touch the Sky told him their names and explained about the fraud by Hiram Steele that had sent them on this long journey southeast. He added that the only way for the Cheyennes to achieve justice would be to expose Steel's similar fraud against the Cherokee Nation—official wards of the U.S. Government.

"Steele's daughter gave me your name," Touch the Sky said. "She told me you might help us. Will you?"

Jack Morningstar was silent for a long time. He stared at his knuckles, scarred from hard work.

"Kristen Steele sent you? You're telling me she knows what you came here to do?"

Touch the Sky nodded. "She's watched me whip Steele before. I swear it on my medicine bundle."

"Kristen Steele," Morningstar said, "is one fine girl. When my wife was dying of the smallpox, Kristen stuck with her to the end. Held her hand, talked to her, prayed with her. Prayed with her, when that stinking Ephraim Long wouldn't even send for the Methodist minister—this, even though the government gave him money for medicines that Hiram Steele never supplied. All we got for smallpox and consumption is Epsom salts and quinine!

"I like that girl. But her father? Hiram Steele is a piece of shit, just like his partner Long. I know I take his money, but a man has to live. I hate that bastard. When the paleskins drove us off our farms back east, as soon as the troops marched us off at bayonet point, white thieves descended on our property like jackals. Took everything. Thieves just like Steele and Long."

Touch the Sky said, "Then you'll help us?"

Morningstar shook his head. "I talk tough, but it ain't that easy, Touch the Sky. I take it you've already locked horns with that ugly son of a bitch Mankiller?"

Touch the Sky nodded. "Granted, he's a mean one, and dangerous as a badger in a barrel. But he's only a man, and he bleeds like the rest."

"The hell he's only a man! He's the devil himself, and I'm damn near convinced no mortal man will ever put him under. He's above the law because he is the law. He just recently killed a man in cold blood for sneaking off the reservation to get drunk. Crushed his neck like a bird egg. He's got a police force of twenty of the meanest Indians west of the Mississippi. Steele and Long can go right on stealing our goods. Hell, they can order us lowly Injuns to piss in a cup and drink it if they want to because they got Mankiller to enforce the orders and keep the complainers scared spitless. Especially now that Long has brought back tithing."

"What's that?"

"Tithing? It's supposed to be illegal now. But who's to stop him? The Long Knives did it back east before they took our land. You pick one Indian out of every ten, make him responsible for any problems with the other nine. A man gets so scared of punishment, he starts to spy on his friends, to report them to the bosses."

Little Horse was anxious to know what was happening. Touch the Sky translated the gist of the conversation so far. Then he switched back to English.

"Seems to me," he said slowly to Morningstar, "like you're really saying that some Cherokees might fight Steele and Long if they stop seeing Mankiller as a little tin god. That they need to see how he and his policemen are not above the law, that they can be punished, too."

"All that's a mighty tall order, Cheyenne. But sure, if that ever happened, Steele and Long would have to call it quits. A rattler ain't shit without its fangs."

"All right then," Touch the Sky said. "We'll start with one of Mankiller's favorite deputies. The meanest one he's got."

"That would be Creek Hater. He'd flay his own mother for a cheap cigar."

"Good. Tell us where to find him."

Just after sunrise the next morning, the Cherokee policeman named Creek Hater packed his drinking jewelry into his saddlebags. That was what Mankiller called them—iron knuckles made from horseshoe nails. All of the Cherokee policemen carried them, but none used them as frequently or eagerly as did Creek Hater.

Creek Hater was patrolling his favorite area, the huge tract of forest along the southern boundary of the reservation. By reservation law—strictly enforced by Ephraim Long and the police—hunting was forbidden. It was the Indian Bureau's intention to discourage the red man's dependence on hunting, to increase his reliance on farming and skilled trades.

But Creek Hater didn't care about the intentions of white fools. All he cared was that this stretch of forest offered good hunting. And though firearms were illegal and scarce on the reservation, bows and arrows were not. With luck he would catch a hunter and have himself a little fun while also earning his pay.

He let his sorrel set its own pace through the trees while he searched left and right for signs of movement. He was detouring around a patch of bog when he spotted movement dead ahead, on the far side of a small clearing.

His horse was trained to stop when the reins touched the ground. Creek Hater threw them down, then quietly slid off his mount. He took his carbine from its boot and removed a coil of rope from his saddle horn. Then he moved silently from tree to tree, working his way around the edge of the clearing.

He spotted movement again, then grinned as he recognized the skinny frame of the youth named Oliver Lame Deer. The boy was still in his teens, and Creek Hater had already caught two of his brothers hunting small game around here.

Creek Hater moved silently for a big man. Oliver had his back to him and was down on one knee behind a tree to aim at a rabbit. Creek Hater waited until the youth had released his arrow and skewered the rabbit. When he stood to retrieve the kill, Creek Hater spoke up.

"Drop the bow and stand real still."

Oliver started, looked quickly back over his shoulder, and turned pale when he recognized the highly feared lawman. Only a few minutes later, the frightened youth was tied tight to the same tree he had hidden behind. Creek Hater ambled over to the dead rabbit, picked it up, and pushed the bloody arrow through. He snapped the shaft so it couldn't be used again. Then he tied the rabbit to his belt. Would be damn good eating later in a stew.

"My family could use that meat," Oliver said. "You're gonna thump on me anyway. Why not least give me the rabbit? Our rations was way short this time, and we ran out of pork in a month."

Creek Hater smiled and walked back to his horse. As he returned, he donned his drinking jewelry. "Bullshit. Your drunken old man traded all the best stuff for grog."

"He tried, sure. But the pork was so putrid this time they wouldn't take it!"

"It's against the law to trade allotment goods. Liquor is illegal, too."

The youth stared back defiantly. "A-huh. That don't stop the policemen from drinking good white man's whiskey."

Creek Hater doubled his iron-reinforced fist and drew it back for a short, hard punch to the ribs. But it never connected—a heartbeat later a menacing voice called out behind him in English:

"Hit him even once, Cherokee, and you cross over today."

Instantly, Creek Hater regretted having returned his carbine to the horse. He turned slowly, expecting a white man. Instead, he confronted the same two Cheyennes the tribal police had almost drowned. The little one held a nasty-looking four-barreled shotgun on him, the tall one a percussion-action Sharps rifle.

"You know I'm a policeman. Kill me and you're in a world of hurt."

"You're a bullying pig," Touch the Sky replied. "A coward who licks the white men's boots and lords it over unarmed Indians. You probably will need killing eventually, but it's going to be your own people who do it, not me. For now, we have other plans for you."

Little Horse cut Oliver Lame Deer loose. The same ropes were now used to secure Creek Hater.

"Stay," Touch the Sky told Oliver, making it an order so Creek Hater wouldn't punish him later. "I want you to see this. And then I want you to spread the word. The red men are united in this battle, all tribes are one. From now on it's open season on Hiram Steele, Ephraim Long, and these criminals who call themselves policemen."

Creek Hater wore his black hair long and loose, proud of his hair as were many Indian men. Touch the Sky moved closer and suddenly grabbed it, wrapping it several times around his wrist and jerking it back hard.

A moment later his knife was in his hand. Creek Hater stared in wide-eyed disbelief.

"No!" Creek Hater shouted. "No!"

His sneering disbelief gave way to cold panic as he realized this crazy Cheyenne fool meant to scalp him!

Chapter Seven

But Touch the Sky did not exactly scalp the brutal policeman.

He and Little Horse had talked it over carefully before they jumped him. It didn't matter how badly hated Mankiller and his brutal deputies were—not if the rest of the Cherokees saw the Cheyenne action as going too far, as interference by outsiders. Most tribes valued intense loyalty to the group as basic to survival in war and other hardships. The proud Cherokees were no exception.

But also like many other tribes, their men took great pride in their long, thick, shiny hair. Most Indians interpreted a mutilation of the hair as a grave insult to the victim's courage and manhood. So the two Cheyennes chose a more effective strategy—they humiliated Creek Hater's character as an individual, not as a Cherokee.

While Little Horse put his knife to work shredding the highly prized campaign hat, badge of the Cherokee police, Touch the Sky chopped Creek Hater's hair. He sawed it off in ragged handfuls, leaving Creek Hater's head looking like a plucked prairie chicken.

The moccasin telegraph was quick on every reservation. Within 48 hours, everyone knew the story about how the bully Creek Hater got his feathers clipped. When Hiram Steele heard the story—first through Ephraim Long, then directly from the sheepish Creek Hater—he had double cause for alarm. For this was not just a serious threat to his control of the reservation. It also meant that his most dangerous enemy in the world was out to defeat him again.

So Steele called an emergency meeting, at his house, with Long and Mankiller. Kristen was impressed into reluctant service as cook and servant. While the reservation Cherokees nearby subsisted on a foul concoction of flour and tripe, Kristen served the three men a dinner of venison steak, beans with bacon, biscuits and butter, apple pudding, and coffee.

But Hiram Steele was irritable and distracted and hardly touched the delicious food.

"I'm telling you right now," Steele said emphatically, looking at Mankiller, "you made a serious mistake when you didn't kill those two."

Mankiller, busy devouring his third mound of pudding, paid no attention to the white man whose money paid his salary. The spoon looked tiny in his huge bear paw.

"A serious mistake," Steele repeated. "Why did you do it?"

Kristen hovered near the table, refilling coffee cups from a blue enamelled pot. Mankiller watched her turn white as bleached bones at her father's question. The wily Cherokee had left her name out when he told her father what happened at Pawnee Creek.

"Any more pudding?" he said quietly to Kristen, and she nodded a bit too quickly, taking his empty bowl and hurrying into the kitchen. Mankiller grinned, enjoying himself.

"I don't get it, Hiram," Long said. "You damn near had kittens the last time you mentioned the Cheyenne. Now you're getting all steamed up over a pair of brazen renegades. Simmer down. If they're foolish enough to hang around here, Mankiller will give them a comeuppance they'll never forget."

Mankiller devoured three biscuits in as many bites, then wiped his fingers on the lace tablecloth. Steele was too distracted to notice.

"Mankiller isn't the issue," Steele said. "It's these goddamn Cheyennes! I'm telling you, I know who they are. The description Mankiller gave fits them like a glove. These ain't just a pair of blanket Indians turned maverick. I can't be sure why they're this far south. But you can write it on your pillowcase—we're up against it now!"

"Hiram, be reasonable, man. There's only two of them."

Steele shook his head violently. "No. No. Don't even think that way. These two can't be counted like other Injuns."

Kristen returned with Mankiller's pudding. "That's the last of it," she told him apologetically.

"'Preciate it. Got any pie or cake?"

She looked startled. "Some blueberry pie, I think."

"That'll do. Some milk'd be real nice, too." He wiped out the pudding in two bites. Kristen returned to the kitchen. Hiram finally seemed to notice that something odd was going on between Mankiller and his daughter. This was one damned uppity Indian, ordering a white girl around like that. But even Steele, who brooked insolence from few men, had no desire to confront Mankiller.

"The thing of it is," Steele said slowly, thinking out loud, "they don't just happen to be here. Not these two. It's damned important to stop them, and pronto."

Kristen returned with a big hunk of pie and a cup of milk for Mankiller. Steele watched her, his eyes squinting shrewdly shut. For the first time he wondered where his daughter was when the Cheyennes had been caught by Mankiller. But before he could ask, Long spoke up.

"On second thought, you may be right, Hiram. Maybe these renegade bucks are up to something besides the usual hell-raising and thieving. This thing with humiliating Creek Hater—it was done deliberately to cast aspersion on the reservation police, to foment the rest to rebellion against my authority."

"Now you've caught the gait! That's what I'm telling you. You and Mankiller have to make it a priority to catch them before this snowballs into something we can't handle."

"Well," Long said, scratching thoughtfully at one of his mutton chops, "if these Cheyenne intruders enjoy playing Robin Hood so much, let's give them another opportunity."

"What do you mean?"

"I've got a plan." Long started to speak, but Steele's eyes cut to the end of the table. Kristen was clearing away serving dishes. Her eyes met her father's.

Steele lifted his hand, stopping Long. Then he looked at his daughter. "That can wait," he told her. "You got something to do up in your room?"

She nodded. Long rose hastily as she left.

"Delicious dinner, Miss Steele," he told her, bowing slightly. "A man could get spoiled by that kind of cooking."

"Not if he gave half a thought to those who aren't eating," she retorted.

Mankiller sat right where he was, picking his front teeth with a thumbnail.

"Pie's a little stale," he told her, belching loudly. He grinned at her confusion and even wider as Hiram Steele again looked at them, befuddled but suspicious.

When the girl was gone, Hiram looked at Long. "All right," he said. "Let's hear this plan of yours."

It was all Kristen could do to keep from collapsing from nervous fear while Mankiller teased her. Her father sensed something. She could tell. Somehow the crafty Cherokee had guessed that she knew the Cheyennes and that her father knew she knew them and didn't like the fact.

As she escaped upstairs to her room, her legs trembled as if she'd just run a long way uphill.

If her father ever found out that she had begged for the Cheyennes' lives, his anger would be too great to tell. Never would she forget his cold, stone-eyed rage and hatred when he had caught Matthew and her together back when they were only sixteen. Her father had already struck her and thrown her to the floor and threatened to disown her as punishment for brief meetings since then. Kristen did not doubt that he was even capable of killing her if he ever found out she was in touch with Matthew again.

And certainly he must be suspicious now. He would be watching her, sticking to her as close as ugly on a buzzard. But she couldn't simply sit back and let her father kill Matthew. And Mankiller—she was beginning to suspect that he only let the Cheyennes go for the sheer pleasure of toying with them again before he killed them. He was insane and brutal, yet crafty as an old fox.

Once in her room, she closed and locked the door. Then she crossed to the cast-iron heating vent near her bed. There was a huge fireplace in the dining room below, and this grate opening in the floor let heat from below into her room. It also, she had already noticed, permitted her to eavesdrop on conversations below.

She lowered herself to the floor and slowly,

inch by inch, opened the vent. Now and then it screeched like a rusty hinge, and she cringed. But eventually it was wide open, and she could easily hear Long's and her father's voices and Mankiller's occasional grunts.

As she listened, slowly comprehending their plan, her nostrils flared in indignant anger. It was a veritable deathtrap they were plotting! Cold-blooded murder, pure and simple. She had to do something.

She thought about her arrangement with Matthew to leave messages under a brick near the shed door. Kristen couldn't be sure how often he checked that spot—nor that he would check in time, should she leave a warning there. But it was the only chance she had to help him and Little Horse.

But how to get the message there? Leaving the house by the front door was out of the question because she would have to pass her father.

She glanced at the window. Could she climb down the lightning rod without breaking her neck? And what if she couldn't climb back up? But she decided she had to try.

Kristen hastily changed into her leather riding pants and a pair of boots, then tied her hair in a ponytail. Next she wrote a quick note to Matthew, folded it, and tucked it into her blouse. Heart pounding loudly in her ears, she crossed to the window and slid it open.

It seemed a long way to the ground, and the dark maw of the night held numerous dangers. But Matthew's life was on the line, and besides, her father and Long were simply wrong. Too many were suffering so that they could live high on the hog. Somebody had to fight them.

Taking a deep breath for courage, feeling very little like a brave hero, the frightened girl lifted one leg over the sill.

"Father, I am frightened for Touch the Sky," Honey Eater said. "For three sleeps in a row now I have dreamed of crows."

Her words startled Arrow Keeper. It was late into the night, and though it was only mildly cool, the ailing shaman had a hot fire blazing in his firepit to warm his old bones. The orange flames emphasized the deep furrow between his eyebrows, the network of seams on his weathered face. Honey Eater's face, in contrast, was taut and flawless, though pinched with worry.

"You, too, little daughter?" he replied. "I, too, have dreamed of death omens. However, when one has as many winters behind him as I, this thing is not unusual."

His smile was meant to comfort her. But Honey Eater was beyond comfort tonight. It was always hard for her when Touch the Sky rode out to face unknown dangers. Black Elk was riding herd guard, but his followers were everywhere. She had sneaked to Arrow Keeper's tipi at great risk.

"Father, you know how Black Elk, Wolf Who Hunts Smiling, and the rest plot against Touch the Sky. Despite everything he has done for his tribe, all his suffering, the blood he has shed, his enemies cleverly keep the pall of doubt over Touch the Sky. Now, with many upset over these worthless goods, they are speaking against him again. And this time, I sense they are close to serious treachery."

Something in her tone, and the urgent look she cast him, alerted Arrow Keeper. "What do you mean, little one? Speak the straight word and shame the Wendigo."

"Father, recently I heard Wolf Who Hunts Smiling tell Black Elk that the only obstacle to banishing Touch the Sky forever is you. I am afraid for him and you."

Arrow Keeper reached one scrawny arm out from under his blanket and patted the girl's shoulder.

"Little Honey Eater, I would speak bent words if I told you your fear is only a thing of smoke. As for Wolf Who Hunts Smiling, his treachery knows no bounds. You are right to fear him. But he will not kill me—my time to cross over is near at hand. And know this. Maiyun, the Good Supernatural, has His own battle plan. No mortal warrior can interfere with that plan."

Honey Eater took a little comfort from these words. "I hope so, Father. As much as I fear Touch the Sky's tribal enemies, I also fear he faces great danger from a powerful enemy without. One who stalks him right now."

Again Arrow Keeper's eyes narrowed thoughtfully as he studied this remarkable girl. Long had he suspected that she, too, possessed a bit of the shaman's hidden eye.

"Daughter, what have you seen?" he asked.

"It sounds foolish, I know, but I have dreamed

of a huge man whose face is all in shadow. Only—"

"Only what, Honey Eater?"

"Only, instead of hands, this big man has eagle's talons. Huge eagle's talons."

A chill moved up Arrow Keeper's spine. It was the same image from his own medicine dream.

Something in his face alerted her. "What is it?" she demanded. "What do you know?"

He shook his head evasively. "Only this," he said. "Maiyun has His own battle plan."

Mankiller moved slowly along the bank of Pawnee Creek, following it south out of Great Bend.

He let his big 16-hand bay set its own pace in the generous light of a full moon. The good dinner he had enjoyed earlier at Hiram Steele's place still lay warm in his belly. The Cherokee sat slumped far forward in the saddle, leaning low first to the left side, then the right. He had eyes like a cat and could read sign in the moonlight.

He encountered fresh horse droppings. Mankiller dismounted and broke them apart to see if they were made by white men's or Indian ponies.

Indian ponies. . . .

His deputies grained their horses and fed them rough forage, so the police horses were ruled out. And though it was allowed, very few Cherokees on the reservation even owned ponies. Those who did seldom rode in this direction.

Mankiller stood up again and adjusted his

broad-brimmed hat. The trap they were setting for the two Cheyennes might work. In case it didn't, Mankiller planned on eventually smoking this pair of foxes out of their den.

He avoided the Indian side when he mounted, swinging up from the left. Then he chucked up his horse and resumed his slow journey, bringing death steadily closer for the two Cheyennes.

Chapter Eight

Fortunately for the Cheyennes, Touch the Sky visited the secret hiding place only hours after Kristen left the note for him.

Kristen's light had been on, and once he even saw her standing in the window. But he knew that he would seriously endanger her if he sneaked up into her room too often. He hadn't really expected any word from her this soon. But after he read her cryptic note, he realized the war was on. Steele knew he was here, and the rabid Indian hater planned to get sweet revenge for that humiliating defeat in Bighorn Falls.

"Clearly," Little Horse said when Touch the Sky had returned to their cavern camp and translated the note, "our little sport with Creek Hater worried the hair-face chiefs. This punishment the note mentions—clearly it is meant to show the folly of challenging Long and Mankiller."

Touch the Sky nodded. "Not only that. It is also meant to flush us out of cover."

Little Horse grinned, recognizing the mischievous glint in his friend's eyes. "Well, brother? Will it flush us out?"

Touch the Sky nodded. "It will. It will also flush out a surprise. Now listen, Cheyenne, for I have a plan."

On the day after Ephraim Long and Hiram Steele hatched their latest plot, a brief notice was posted throughout the Cherokee reservation. It was also published in the weekly reservation newspaper.

A NOTICE TO ALL MEMBERS OF THE CHEROKEE NATION: RESPECT FOR THE LAW OF THE LAND IS ESSENTIAL TO GOOD GOVERNMENT. REPEATED VIOLATIONS OF RESERVATION LAWS AND OPEN ACTS OF DISRESPECT TOWARD RESERVATION POLICE HAVE NECESSITATED THE FOLLOWING PROCLAMATION: ON MONDAY, MAY 12, AT NOON, AN HABITUAL VIOLATOR OF RESERVATION LAW WILL BE PUBLICLY WHIPPED AT THE CEREMONIAL SQUARE ADJACENT TO AGENT LONG'S RESIDENCE. SUCH PUBLIC DISCIPLINARY MEASURES WILL CONTINUE UNTIL LAW AND ORDER PREVAIL ON THE RESERVATION.

Knowing morbid curiosity would draw more Indians, Long deliberately omitted naming the habitual violator or his supposed crimes. The desire to know who the unfortunate victim was would fetch the Cherokees, he thought. With luck, it would also lure the Cheyennes.

One day before the public whipping was scheduled, the youth named Oliver Lame Deer went out spear-fishing as usual.

The ban against hunting was strictly enforced, but fishing was still permitted and widely practiced. The Cherokees had been famous spear-fishers back east of the river called Great Waters. Those who survived the deadly forced migration known as the Cherokee Trail of Tears brought their skills to the West.

Oliver had a favorite spot on Pawnee Creek where bass and bluegill and trout were plentiful. Not only did his skill supplement his large family's meager diet, but some of the catch would be smoked on wooden drying racks and swapped for badly needed trade items.

Like many others on the reservation, Oliver had been heartened by these mysterious Cheyennes who sheared Creek Hater's hair. Now a few of the leaders on the reservation—skilled tradesmen like Jack Morningstar—were firing up the people. Still, Mankiller and his deputies were no Indians to trifle with.

Oliver thought all of these things as he lay patiently on his stomach, staring down the steep bank into the swift-moving current of Pawnee Creek. His three-tined spear was balanced in his right hand. Something flashed in the water below. He drew his arm back and tried to throw, but the spear wouldn't move!

More confused than frightened, he looked back to see what had caught it. His eyes went big when they met Mankiller's. The huge policeman gripped his spear.

"You're under arrest," he said.

"For what, Mankiller? Fishing is not illegal!"

"No. But stealing corn from the reservation garden is."

Oliver blinked. "What? I haven't been around the gardens since I drew hoeing detail. What are you—"

Mankiller lay the wooden spear against his knee and snapped it as easily as a dry twig. He threw both pieces into the water.

"I said you stole corn from the reservation garden. I caught you in the act. Me and Creek Hater."

Now Oliver understood. It didn't matter that the Cheyenne had ordered him to stay when Creek Hater was humiliated. Because he had witnessed Creek Hater's hair being razed, he had been selected for the public beating.

"I won't beg," he said. "It's not fair and you know it. But I ain't begging. You've whipped me and my brothers plenty just because we ain't impressed when you play the big Indian."

Mankiller whacked his boot with his quirt. The hand holding the rawhide quirt seemed as big as a pannier. "I whipped you plenty, and I plan on whipping you plenty more. I don't play nothing, tadpole. I am a big Indian."

Several miles east of the settlement of Great Bend, a huge, grassy meadow formed a tree-bordered park on the reservation. This was the central gathering place for religious ceremonies. It was also the site of the official residence of the Cherokee Agent, Ephraim Long, whose large fieldstone house stood on one flank of the meadow.

Indians were gathering in scattered groups, milling near a huge oak tree that stood by itself in the grass. There were children, elders, and young women with bear grease in their hair and babies in backboards. The policemen, conspicuous in their hook-and-eye hats, controlled the people and kept them from getting too close to the tree.

Many cast hateful glances at the mounted policemen, but few said anything. Names of complainers ended up on lists and their allotment goods could mysteriously disappear. Still, several grinned or stifled laughs when they spotted Creek Hater wearing an old slouch hat to disguise his new haircut.

The most conspicuous guest was the stern-jawed Hiram Steele. He stood by himself, proudly remote from the Indians around him. Oliver Lame Tree stood near the tree, his eyes fearful but defiant. It had not been necessary to tie him up. Mankiller had put Uncle Sam's watch and chain on the prisoner: a six-foot chain and an iron ball weighing 25 pounds. The chain was attached to the youth's skinny ankle by an iron band.

Ephraim Long came out of his house and crossed the meadow to address the crowd, speaking from a hastily erected wooden platform. The policemen maintained silence while Long deplored the lack of law and order on the reservation. He also warned the Cherokee people about the dangers of outside agitators from uncivilized tribes, pagans who would interfere with tribal unity and authority. At one point he stared directly at the cooper, Jack Morningstar, a known malcontent. Morningstar matched his stare.

While Long delivered his spiel, Mankiller repeatedly cast his glance toward the thick stand of trees behind them, then toward a long spine of rocks that nearly split the meadow.

If trouble came, Mankiller told himself, it would come from those trees. But Mankiller, too, had a little surprise in store.

He glanced toward the rocky spine and grinned with pleasant anticipation. Whoever emerged from those trees must pass the spine.

Long finally wound up his speech and nodded at Mankiller. The police chief dismounted and took a knotted-thong whip from his saddlebag. He cracked it a few times as he crossed toward the tree.

He squared off, planted his feet, and cracked the whip again for good measure. The crowd went as silent as a burial forest. Mankiller raised one arm and drew it back.

"Hi-ya! Hi-ya!"

It wasn't clear where the Cheyenne war cry came from. But there could be no mistaking the buckskin-clad warrior bearing down on them! Clearly, from the warrior's lance and headdress and his pinto mustang, this was one of the Cheyennes currently plaguing them. Mankiller laughed in open delight, waiting until the attacker came abreast of the rock spine.

Then Mankiller drew the Remington pistol from his sash and fired an offhand shot.

This was the prearranged signal to the six Cherokee policemen who had been held in reserve, hiding behind the rock spine. As one they rose and drew a bead on the Cheyenne, carefully avoiding the valuable pony.

Their rifles cracked, the Cheyenne flew from the saddle and landed sprawling in the dirt. The frightened mount turned and bolted for the trees again. The police had dismounted when Mankiller did. Now they raised a triumphant shout and raced on foot toward the fallen Cheyenne. Long and Steel trailed them at a run.

Mankiller's face creased in an ear-to-ear smile. The plan had worked beautifully! He was still clearing a hole in the bystanders when the first angry shouts went up from his men.

Mankiller literally threw several people aside, then stared down at the Cheyenne in the grass. They had been foxed again. The victim was merely a buckskin suit filled with grass, complete with a crude headdress and lance!

Rage sent hot blood into Mankiller's face. But the foxes weren't finished quite yet. Steele raised an angry shout of warning.

He pointed back toward the clearing. The police horses were all gathered there, hobbled. But one of the Cheyennes had sneaked out from the opposite tree line and slipped their hobbles while the crowd was distracted. Now the Cheyenne fired his shotgun, and the horses scattered at the resounding blast.

"Goddamn it!" Steele screamed at the top of his lungs. "Catch those bastards! Chase 'em!"

But few in the crowd seemed at all inclined to capture these brave and reckless Cheyenne intruders. As for the policemen, they were too busy trying to chase down their horses.

Chapter Nine

"I told you," Hiram Steele said, fuming. "Didn't I by God tell you those two meant trouble? What they dished up yesterday was just a taste."

Steele was so distracted and angry that he had neglected to touch his Scotch. Mankiller kept a steady eye on Steele's full glass from his side of the table. Ephraim Long cocked his head in curiosity and watched his business partner closely.

"I don't get it, Hiram. Those Cheyennes are giving you a fit. You said you ran into them before. All right. But why are you taking ignorant aboriginals so damn personally? What's this bad blood between you and them?"

Steele's eyes cut away evasively. He wasn't about to confess that his own daughter had once been sweet on a full-blood Cheyenne—

hell, might still be. That she had hung on him and kissed him and God knew what else. His glance went to the kitchen, where Kristen was rustling up a quick supper for this hastily arranged meeting. Again the suspicion cankered deep inside him. Had she warned those two Cheyennes about the trap? By God, if she had. . . .

"The details ain't important," he replied. "Just mark my words. Those two spell real bad trouble, the worst kind."

Long picked at some lint on his coat sleeve. "Well, that little dog-and-pony show they put on yesterday was trouble enough for me, all right. I heard a few of the Cherokees cheer when the deputies had to chase their horses down. This kind of thing is dangerous. I've worked hard to teach these savages some discipline, to put the fear of God in them. These damn upstart Cheyennes could get us caught in the middle of a nasty rebellion."

"Now you're reading the sign! That's what I been trying to tell you. We got to blow out their lamps and quick. When it comes down to busting caps, the red men will all side together against the white man every time."

Steele's eyes cut to Mankiller. The huge Cherokee was still staring at his employer's full glass.

"You gonna drink that?" Mankiller said.

Startled, Steele knuckled the glass across the table to Mankiller. "Kristen! Bring the liquor in."

Long rose gallantly when the pretty girl

entered, skirts rustling, and set the cut-glass carboy on the table.

Steele watched her closely, suspicion again narrowing his eyes. She paled under the stare. She met Mankiller's eyes and the Cherokee winked intimately. The girl flushed and hurried back into the kitchen. Steele's anger at this brazen savage's behavior toward a white woman gave way again to nagging doubt. What did he have on her?

"Anyway," Steele said, looking at Long and Mankiller, "it's so important to stop these Cheyennes that I'm putting up good color. To be exact, one thousand in double-eagle gold pieces to the man who kills them and brings me proof."

Mankiller suddenly lost the bored glaze over his eyes. "One thousand for both of them?"

"For both of them. You won't get one without the other, believe me."

"The reservation Indians don't have firearms," Long said. "But I'll spread the word among the whites I know."

Mankiller polished off his Scotch, stood up, and clapped his broad-brimmed hat on his head.

"Don't bother," he said. "That money is mine."

The Cherokee skilled tradesmen had their own lodge on the reservation—a large, one-room cabin with crude plank tables and backless benches. On the night after the bold Cheyenne raid, Jack Morningstar wandered down to visit with some of his lodge brothers. The talk, naturally, centered on the mysterious Cheyenne strangers.

"Who the hell are they?" said a burly, middle-aged blacksmith who called himself Captain Bill.

"Who cares?" said a cobbler from the Virginia River Clan. "They're making life hard for the whiteskins who steal from us. They're welcome here."

Morningstar had still not mentioned to the rest his visit from the Cheyennes. Now he glanced quickly around to make sure none of Mankiller's men was present.

"They're fighting for us," he said. "That's more'n I can say for us."

Several heads turned to stare at him. Morningstar was not one to speak in riddles.

"What do you mean?" Captain Bill said.

Morningstar shrugged his shoulders. "Look at it. Ain't their reservation. Ain't their battle. But they're fighting it anyway."

"Hell," the cobbler said. His name was Otto and, like Morningstar, he wore white men's machine-made clothing. "My father and my uncle both died fighting the Creeks. I got their war shields, and they're plenty scarred up."

"I've seen them," Captain Bill said. "Your clan was all warriors back in the Ohio River country. So was mine. My grandfather died defending his grist mill when the Long Knives came to take it. My grandma fell at his side."

"Any of us can make brags on our ancestors," Morningstar said casually. "Point is, them Cheyennes're fighting for us now, and all we're doing is sitting on our duffs talking about past bravery."

"So what can we do?" the cobbler demanded.

Morningstar shrugged as if all this were merely a speculative game, not a real plan of action. "We've got some horses in the common corral. We got axes, bows and arrows, and knives. We could, say, draw straws. See who rides with the Cheyennes."

"Rides with 'em? Rides where?"

"Well, for instance," Morningstar said, "Steele's got a new shipment coming in day after tomorrow. It'll be going to his warehouse on Exposition Street in town."

"That's where he stores the shoddy goods," Captain Bill said.

Morningstar nodded. "Sure. He stockpiles them there. But what if a raiding party met the freighters north of town and destroyed all that crap?"

A long silence followed this suggestion. Resentment against Steele, Long, and Mankiller ran deep—even among these skilled tradesmen, who were better off than most on the reservation. But years of hopeless suffering had dulled their fighting instincts.

"Even if I didn't think it's a foolish plan," Otto said, "how in the hell would we get wind of it to those Cheyennes?"

Morningstar held his face impassive, not revealing his elation. Clearly his lodge brothers were more willing to fight than he had believed. Watching those young Cheyennes yesterday had inspired them. All it needed was one spark—the fighting Cheyennes from the north country—to perhaps set this hotbed of misery ablaze. He had agreed to meet the Cheyennes again this evening. Now he could surprise them with some potentially encouraging news.

"Don't worry about that," he replied. "They ain't far away."

Less than 48 hours after the discussion in the tradesmen's lodge, five riders forded Pawnee Creek well north of the settlement of Great Bend: Touch the Sky, Little Horse, Jack Morningstar, Captain Bill, and Otto.

Only the two Cheyennes were equipped with firearms. The Cherokees each had powerful osage bows and a few axes lashed to their mounts. The Cherokees' horses were far from prime horseflesh: swayback draft animals liberated from the small common corral.

"You see like an eagle. Drop behind and watch our back trail, brother," Touch the Sky told Little Horse. "Make sure Mankiller or his deputies have not cut sign on us or spotted us leaving."

With Jack Morningstar pointing out the way, this unlikely war party followed the deep-seamed freight road that bore north toward the storage docks at Fort Hays. The teamsters hauling Steele's goods were due to reach Great Bend late this morning. Touch the Sky intended, however, to intercept them well outside of town.

"They're sure as hell gonna have armed guards," Morningstar said. "At least two. And the teamsters will be armed, prob'ly with scatterguns. But they won't be expecting trouble. Most of the Indian flare ups are west of here."

113

Touch the Sky nodded. "Don't forget, no blood-letting if we can avoid it. We've got no quarrels with these freighters. It's the cargo we want to attack."

Several miles farther north, Little Horse caught up to the rest. "All clear," he reported. "No one is trailing us yet."

The five Indians rode in a loose skirmish line, the sound of hoofclops and bit rings from the Cherokee mounts the only noise. To their right, the morning sun tracked higher, looking like a dull yellow ball; to their left the plains rolled on, unbroken brown, until lost in the haze on the far horizon. Now and then one of the Cherokees would catch a companion's eye and grin self-consciously. Despite their tribe's warrior legacy, these Cherokees had seen little combat.

"Brothers!" said the sharp-eyed Little Horse, pointing north. "Look there!"

Straight ahead, little dust puffs rose above the horizon.

Touch the Sky felt a familiar humming in his blood. The battle was close upon them! He pointed to a long ridge on their left.

"All right! Cherokees, you know the plan! Take cover behind the crest of that ridge. Have your fire arrows ready. Little Horse and I will do the rest. When your last arrow is spent, return to the point where we forded the Pawnee."

He and Little Horse angled their ponies off to the right and chucked them up to a canter, keeping first a line of cedars, then a low bluff between them and the approaching pack train. Touch the Sky was following the advice of old

Chief Yellow Bear, who had spoken to him from the Land of Ghosts during his Medicine Lake vision quest. *When all seems lost, become your enemy.*

Touch the Sky's plan was simple and based on one of the bluecoat's favorite battle strategies: the pincers movement. It was up to him and Little Horse to nudge that supply train closer to the ridge. Once the wooden wagons were easy targets, the Cherokees would get a chance to demonstrate their marksmanship.

They cleared the bluff, the supply train now easily visible on their left flank. There were a half-dozen mule-team wagons and, as Jack Morningstar had predicted, an armed guard riding in front, another in the rear. Both men carried Henry rifles, noted for accuracy at long distances.

"Charge them!" Touch the Sky said in Cheyenne to Little Horse. "We will count coup on the guards. Do not ride in a straight line or they will lead us and shoot plumb. We have got to get them nervous enough to swerve well right."

"Hi-ya!" Little Horse shouted. "Hi-ya, hii-ya!"

They dug their knees into their ponies' flanks and surged forward. The two friends split wide, Touch the Sky angling toward the front guard, Little Horse the rear. They crouched low over their well-trained ponies' necks, making small targets. They also ran in a carefully practiced zigzagging charge, frustrating the guards with the long rifles.

Touch the Sky felt his calico mustang straining beneath him, the damp foam against his skin, and the wind streaming in his loose black locks. He bore down on his man, divots of dirt flying behind his pony's hoofs. He could see the drivers hastily snatching up their weapons, the armed guards squaring off to meet the attack.

He surged closer, his man fired, and a bullet whirred past Touch the Sky's ear. The guard hastily began recharging his piece. Shouting a triumphant war cry, Touch the Sky cracked his lance down hard on the hindquarters of the other man's horse. For good measure, and to heighten the panic, he drew his Sharps from its boot and snapped off a round over the head of the lead driver. The mules and horses in the remuda were bucking, jack-knifing, and crow-hopping, threatening to break loose from the string.

Now he and Little Horse faded back a bit and faked another charge. As they had hoped, the wagons veered right, but the lead teamster did not order them into a circular defense. They had decided to wage a running battle and race for Great Bend before the rest of the wild Indians showed up for a possible massacre.

The rest came off exactly as planned.

The three Cherokees had only one battle assignment: to pepper those freight wagons with fire arrows. And they performed magnificently. Before the nervous whites knew what had hit them, dozens of flaming arrows had hit their wooden wagons.

Now the two Cheyennes went into action again. Each time a teamster tried to put out a fire, Touch the Sky or Little Horse sent a bullet or deadly, flint-tipped arrow within inches of them. This was risky, forcing them to skyline themselves to aim—the armed guards returned dangerous fire.

But soon, the mission was a fiery, smoke-belching success. None of the teamsters had been injured. But four of the six wagons were burning beyond control, and the other two were substantially damaged.

Well after Hiram Steele and Ephraim Long had fallen asleep that night, both men were startled awake by the sound of shattering glass. Both nerve-frazzled men also found a note wrapped around the rock that broke their windows.

Make good on your legal obligations to the red man, or the harassment campaign continues!

Chapter Ten

Mankiller led his big, 16-hand bay slowly along Pawnee Creek, scouring the earth for the slightest sign of the two Cheyennes.

He knew they must have a base camp near here. That daring raid yesterday finally proved that. True, none of the teamsters had gotten a close look at the Indians who actually fired arrows on them from behind the ridge. But they had recognized the two boldest bucks as Northern Cheyennes.

And if they had a camp near here, Pawnee Creek was the most likely spot. No other place offered enough shelter or water for ponies. Besides, what little sign he had managed to cut so far had been found near the creek.

One thousand dollars in double-eagle gold pieces. Mankiller could almost feel the weight of

Hiram Steele's bounty money in his saddlebags. With such a stake, a man could set himself up as one hell of a big Indian. Lord it around like Steele and Long, smoke big cigars, wear fancy coats as Chief Red Jacket did.

He felt his huge palms itching as he thought about the sheer pleasure of feeling those Cheyenne necks snap like reeds in his powerful grip. Nobody made a fool of Mankiller and lived to brag on it to his children.

Suddenly the bay lifted its head high, pricked its ears forward. Mankiller stared ahead toward a sharp bend in the creek. The trees and thickets grew dense all along here.

The bay snorted. Mankiller slowly, silently slid to the ground. They were close; he sensed it now. Relying on an old Indian trick, he pinched the bay's nostrils to keep it from whinnying. Then he slid the Remington from his sash and moved slowly forward.

"By now," Little Horse said, "both Long and Steele have received the talking paper you made for them and wrapped around the rocks. They understand our terms."

Touch the Sky nodded. The afternoon was late and the two friends sat in the dense cover just outside the entrance to their cave. Their ponies were hobbled out of sight behind the cave. After dark they would water them, then tether them in the open grass to graze.

"About Long, I know nothing," Touch the Sky said. "What manner of man he is, what kind of fighting fettle he has. As for Steele, expect more

119

hard fighting, although he will pay others to do it for him. He knows our terms, yes. But knowing is not accepting."

While he spoke, Touch the Sky felt a strange prickling of his skin—his shaman sense warning him that something was amiss. He glanced carefully around. Nearby, a badger burrowed a tunnel in the grassy bank of the creek. A stone's throw to his left, a rabbit nibbled at tender new shoots. Overhead, a jay chattered madly. Seeing all this made him relax a bit.

"From what you have told me," Little Horse said, "it sounds clear that Long is the important one. He is the big chief on the reservation. If we can turn his liver white with fear, perhaps he will stop doing business with Steele."

The prickling sensation was back, goose-bumping Touch the Sky's skin. He glanced around. The badger still worked furiously at its tunnel; the rabbit still nibbled at shoots; the jay still chattered overhead.

"Perhaps," he finally answered. "But Steele is not one for giving others a voice in the decision."

All this talk made Touch the Sky recall the letter Kristen had given him—the incriminating letter Steele had written to Long, but never delivered. It was tucked into his parfleche. He had read it so many times he had it memorized. Could he ever put it to good use against the arrogant, Indian-hating Steele? That could happen if—

Suddenly, the badger scurried away to cover. The rabbit dashed off deep into the trees. The jay flew off from its branch.

Fear iced Touch the Sky's veins as he realized that some danger was closing in on them—a danger that he also sensed it was best to avoid.

"Brother," he said urgently to Little Horse, "let us catch up our ponies and ride out of here for a time."

Little Horse cocked his head in curiosity, about to ask why. Then he saw the fear in this young shaman's face, and he understood that the hand of the supernatural was in this thing.

A few heartbeats later, the two Cheyenne braves had disappeared in the thick growth surrounding them.

"I'm tellin' you the straight," Steele said. "It's gone too far. You read the note. That buck means to whack the cork on us! Either you do like I tell you, or we're soon out of business. We can't back off now. We got to corral these Cheyennes while the gate's still open."

Ephraim Long seemed unconvinced. "I'm not so sure, Hiram. What if this whole damn thing curdles on us? You heard those teamsters describe the attack. There were other Indians hiding behind the ridge. What if they were reservation Indians?"

"That's the point, damn it. Give an Injun an inch, he wants the whole rope. You get icy boots, and these savages will end up pissing on your grave."

Long still looked reluctant. "If the newspapers back east were ever to—"

"To hell with the goddamn Indian lovers and

cowardly Quakers!" Steele exploded. "These godless savages didn't even know about the wheel until the white man showed 'em! You do what I told you, or it's coming down to the nut cuttin'!"

Finally Long nodded. "All right. You're not one to panic over nothing. I'll put the word out today."

Steele nodded. "That's the gait. Remember, make it clear you're punishing only those few Cherokees who cheered loudest when the Cheyenne renegades disrupted the whipping. You—"

The stairwell door opened and Kristen entered. Steele quickly shut up. Long rose and gallantly bowed. Kristen ignored him.

"Well," Hiram said with the false joviality that always made Kristen shudder, "here's the very girl! Ephraim was just telling me that he has written out his funding request for that new reservation school we talked about. He's submitting your name for the girls' teacher."

"How nice. And I'll bet that, since you'll have so many accounts with the school anyway, my salary could just be paid directly to you?"

Steele poured a little more enamel into his smile. "That would be sensible, wouldn't it? I pay the bills around here."

His smile made her nervous. Kristen knew he was suspicious of her. If he found out she was in touch with Matthew Hanchon—The thought sent a shiver up her spine.

When she was gone, Long looked at Steele. Something had been bothering him since that rock crashed through his window.

"Hiram? This Cheyenne buck you say wrote the notes. How in the hell does he come to know English well enough to write it down?"

Steele waved the question off impatiently.

"Hell, does it matter? You can learn a dog to walk on its hind legs, too, but it's still a dog. All you need to keep in mind about this Injun is that he needs killing and needs it bad."

On the day following the meeting between Steele and Long, Steele got his way. Several Cherokees were publicly whipped by Mankiller and his deputies.

Touch the Sky and Little Horse learned of the beatings that same day from an angry Jack Morningstar. Once again Touch the Sky decided on retaliation with lightning speed.

"Perhaps you were right after all, brother," he told Little Horse. "Perhaps we should take the fight to Long, too, not just Steele. I think we should visit his lodge this very night."

The Cheyennes already knew, from talks with Morningstar and others, that Long lived alone in his big two-story home, where an old Indian woman cooked and cleaned for him during the day. Since the trouble with the Cheyennes had begun, a Cherokee policeman stayed on guard in the yard throughout the night.

Touch the Sky and Little Horse rode out well after dark. It was a moonless, overcast night, and safe movement was easy. They picketed their ponies well back from the house.

The stone building rose up before them,

looming, still, and dark. Armed only with their knives, they crept close to the house, moving with gusts of wind to cover their noise.

"Brother!" Little Horse whispered, touching his arm. "There is the guard."

Both Cheyennes knelt behind a clump of elderberry bushes at one side of the house. They watched the policeman slowly walk around the house, his carbine at sling arms.

"We can avoid him. But I would feel better," Touch the Sky whispered back, "if he were not wandering about."

Little Horse took his meaning. Again the guard circled the house. Little Horse, famous in his clan for his ability to mimic animals, whimpered like a frightened young puppy.

The guard stopped and stared over toward the bushes. Cherokees were famous for liking dogs. Little Horse whimpered again. The guard walked closer.

He poked behind the bush. Touch the Sky rose behind him and whacked him in the temple with the solid bone handle of his knife. The guard folded to the ground as if he'd been pole-axed. They took his carbine and ammunition, then tied his ankles and wrists with rawhide whangs.

Locks on doors were practically unheard of on the frontier. At the front door the two Cheyennes found the latch string out. They slipped inside the big house and found themselves in a dark, silent room with a big grandfather clock ticking loudly from one corner.

"Brother," Little Horse whispered nervously,

"what is that noise like a heart beating?"

"The white man's time-counter. It will not hurt you."

They moved quickly throughout the entire ground floor, making sure Long was not downstairs.

"Follow me, brother," Touch the Sky whispered, angling toward a staircase near the front door. "He must be upstairs."

Touch the Sky had ascended perhaps five or six steps when he heard a nervous call behind him.

"Brother! What is this? Come back down here!"

Curious, he returned to the bottom of the steps.

"Brother," Little Horse said, "what are you doing? What is this thing?"

Touch the Sky was confused. Little Horse was pointing at the risers of the stairway. Then, all of a moment, he remembered a curious bit of information his friend Old Knobby had told him. Most Plains Indians could not climb steps or ladders, never having even seen them! But this was not the time for Little Horse's first lesson, he decided.

"Just wait here, brother," he said. "Another guard may show up, or Long might come in. I will look around upstairs."

Quietly, wincing every time a stair creaked, Touch the Sky went up to the top floor. The hallway was dark, but a straight seam of light, under one door, told him where Long must be. He slipped forward, moccasins silent on the bare wood floor, and gripped the latch.

The door mewed when he opened it, and Long looked up at him from a writing desk, where he sat making entries in a ledger.

The agent turned several shades paler in the light of a coal-oil lamp. The wild Indian crossing toward him gripped a nasty-looking knife and looked hell-bent on using it.

Touch the Sky saw he was unarmed and stopped.

"Who in the hell are you?" Long said.

"No friend of yours, Long. Nor of Hiram Steele's either."

"Your English is good."

"Good enough to tell you to your face that you're a thief, Agent Long."

"You're talking to a white man, John."

Touch the Sky's muscles danced as his right hand tightened on the knife. "Call me John again, hair face, and I'll be talking to a dead white man."

Long moved all at once, lifting his right foot and slipping the two-shot muff gun out in an eyeblink.

"All right, John. Drop the knife. Then turn and walk back downstairs slowly. We're going to see what you did to that guard out there. If he's dead, you just killed a ward of the U. S. Government, John."

Long held the lamp high behind Touch the Sky, throwing a shimmering pool of light down the stairs as they descended. Touch the Sky spoke loudly in English so Little Horse would hear two voices and know they were coming.

"What are you going to do with me?"

Long's laugh was high-pitched and loud. Power surged in his fingertips. He'd captured a real, by God wild Injun!

"Don't feel so frisky now, do you? Thought you were going to lead all of my Indians back to the blanket, didn't you? Well—*oomph!*"

Long went down hard when Little Horse smashed a ladder-back chair over his head, splintering it. Touch the Sky checked his neck pulse: still strong. The man was out, but not seriously hurt.

"Good thing, brother, you cannot climb stairs!" Touch the Sky ran back upstairs and sat for a moment at the writing desk. Before the two braves slipped out of the house again, Touch the Sky had pinned a note to the unconscious agent's vest.

> *Either clear out or start living up to your legal obligations as a Cherokee agent. Otherwise, you're a dead man.*

Chapter Eleven

"Hiram, it's easy for you to stick to your guns," Ephraim Long said. "It's no skin off your ass if I'm scalped. Before you go issuing so damn many hard orders to others, ask yourself if you'd be willing to carry them out. That savage could have killed me instead of just knocking me out."

Steele was so agitated he had risen from the table and now paced the room, staring at Long. The agent had a nasty, egg-size swelling near the top of one of his muttonchops, where the chair had struck him.

"Long, have you been grazin' loco weed? No skin off my ass? Do you know how much freight I lost in that attack? True, it was inexpensive goods. But you don't have to swallow the loss and pay them riled-up freighters to replace ruined wagons.

"And do you know how much I lost in Wyoming fighting those two renegades? Not to mention what I—we—stand to lose if you get snow in your boots now."

"Wyoming," Long grumbled. "Seems to me you're always licking old wounds instead of looking to avoid new ones. I say we negotiate with these two and see if—"

"Negotiate? In a pig's ass!" Steele exploded. "I want those criminal sons of bitches dead."

"That's just how you're gunna get 'em," Mankiller said quietly, adding a fifth spoonful of sugar to his cup of coffee. His finger was too thick to slip through the china handle, so he was forced to pick the cup up like a bowl. "I've damn near located their camp."

"Good. I'll have the gold in your hands before their bodies turn cold," Steele promised him.

"What you two work out privately is your business," Long said. "But I'm going my own way. Nothing personal, Hiram. But something tells me that tall Cheyenne buck meant exactly what he told me."

"How 'bout you, Chief?" Steele said to Red Jacket. "You throwin' in with me or Agent Long here?"

As if to emphasize his point, Steele pushed a platter of fresh-baked currant scones toward the Cherokee leader, who grinned and helped himself to another, dunking it in his coffee.

"We Cherokees have a saying. 'Only a fool sells his best mule,'" Red Jacket said. "I have no mules for sale."

Steele nodded enthusiastically. The wily

129

chief's meaning was clear. Steele looked at Mankiller.

"How 'bout you, Sheriff? Whose colors you flying?"

Mankiller sucked his cup dry in one long sip. He lifted a corner of the tablecloth and wiped his mouth. "I'm flying the color of gold," he finally replied.

Steele looked at Long, his eyes bright with triumph.

"Everybody's cards are on the table, pard. Do I deal you in or out?"

Long looked confused, like a man just waking up from a long drunk. He glanced at Chief Red Jacket and Mankiller.

"Now hold on here a minute, you two. I'm the agent. How can you two talk about siding with Hiram?"

"'Cuz he's got gold," Mankiller said promptly. "And you ain't. That's how."

"It's a private treaty," Red Jacket added. "You only handle government treaties."

Coffee always put Red Jacket in a loquacious mood. Now he swelled up importantly.

"We Cherokees were proud hunters and farmers back in our ancient homeland. We always liked the Americans. It was the crafty British and Spanish who incited us to war against your people. But I have always admired the whiteskins. True, they exposed my people to smallpox, tuberculosis, syphilis, and measles—"

"That's a real nice speech, Chief," Steele said impatiently. He was still staring at Long. "How 'bout it, Ephraim? You mounting on the left side with us or on the Indian side?"

Long saw it all spelled out, clear as a blood spoor in new snow. Steele was telling him to do what he wished, but he'd best be prepared to die the first time he crossed him. Having Red Jacket on his side meant little. But Mankiller was feeding at Steele's trough, too. That meant plenty.

"Can we strike a deal?" Long said. "You and I will continue with most of our present business arrangements. But I will also appease the Indians somewhat. I want to lift the ban on hunting and scrap the tithing system—that kind of thing."

"Hell," Steele said, "I don't care about that. You got a deal. Just don't go hog wild and promise any changes with the allotment goods. That arrangement stays the same. Beside—"

Steele glanced toward the door to the stairwell. This time Kristen had been sent out of the house on errands while the men talked business. Steele was convinced now that she was eavesdroping somehow, that she was in touch somehow with Matthew Hanchon. And now he was hatching a new plan—one using his daughter as a lure to trap the Cheyenne.

"Besides," Steele said, "I got a gut hunch we'll soon be eliminating the major source of our trouble."

Honey Eater's dream was repeated three nights in a row, which gave it the force of a vision.

She saw herself kneeling in front of Touch the

131

Sky's tipi. She was holding their special stone, the piece of marble on which he had sworn his eternal love. Tears streamed from her eyes, and she knew she was crying because Touch the Sky had ridden off to face unknown dangers, perhaps never to return.

Always, as the dream started, the entrance flap of his tipi was closed tight. But then, glancing up through her tears, she spotted a sight that made her heart leap into her throat. The flap was up now, and inside was Touch the Sky with a sun-haired whiteskin woman in his arms!

Each time Honey Eater would cry out, and each time the pretty whiteskin would stare outside at her with mocking eyes. But then came the worst omen of all. The sound of rapid hoofclops approached behind her, there was a wild nickering, and then Honey Eater would whirl to face a huge, wild-eyed black stallion, its skeleton rider grinning at her from a death's skull.

As always, Honey Eater started awake, drenched in her own sweat. She sat up in the heaped buffalo robes. Her breathing was rapid and shallow. It was dark in the tipi, the fire in the pit having burned down to mere glowing embers. She realized Black Elk was not beside her, and her first reaction was relief. She could be alone with her thoughts.

Then she heard it. Faint, like the noise heard when one was half asleep: the murmur of men's voices out behind the tipi.

Now she recalled. She had dropped off to sleep early, after preparing Black Elk's evening meal.

He, as usual, had wandered off to spend most of his night in the camp clearing, betting on pony races and wrestling matches. He must have returned with some of his friends. The meat racks out behind Black Elk's tipi were a favorite meeting place when trouble was afoot.

Moving quietly, Honey Eater rose and crossed to the back of the tipi. There was a spot where she could roll the hide cover partway up one of the lodge poles and peer outside. She did so now, reminding herself that Black Elk would surely bob her nose if he ever caught her.

"Cousin," Wolf Who Hunts Smiling said, "faint hearts never led a tribe to victory. This Touch the Sky, whom I call White Man Runs Him, again he has ridden out with Little Horse. And once again they have done so without benefit of a council meeting.

"When will you finally read the sign? He has beguiled Arrow Keeper, Chief Gray Thunder, and now even the Star Chamber. Because of him our tribe has gone easy on the paleface intruders. We have even accepted a peace price to let Caleb Riley's miners run all over our hunting grounds. Who knows what treachery White Man Runs Him is up to with hair faces even now?

"It is time for new, younger leaders to force-fully rescue our tribe from this downward path of licking white men's boots."

Wolf Who Hunts Smiling had always been a fiery, effective speaker. Though Black Elk was older, and their battle chief, he nodded once to acknowledge the truth of these words.

"Besides," Swift Canoe added slyly, knowing Black Elk's jealous wrath, "this tall pretend Cheyenne seeks to put on the old moccasin with our married women. Even a man's wife is not safe around him."

A small fire blazed in a circle of stones, outlining their features in a cerise glow. Black Elk's sewn-on ear looked like a flap of tanned leather.

"These things you say ring true enough," Black Elk said. "I trained him. He is a good warrior—as good as any I have seen, and perhaps even the best. But he is not straight-arrow Cheyenne to the quick of him. In his heart he still wears white man's shoes. He carries the white stink for life. He preaches cooperation with those who would exterminate the red man."

"Besides this," said Medicine Flute, a sleepy-eyed, slender brave who claimed to have the gift of visions, "he cleverly sets himself up as a shaman. In this ruse he is assisted by Arrow Keeper, who dotes on him in his frosted years."

"Arrow Keeper," Wolf Who Hunts Smiling said, his furtive eyes constantly in motion, "is tottering on his funeral scaffold. He, at least, will soon be gone. Then White Man Runs Him will have lost his best ally."

"And then," Medicine Flute said, "the tribe will be without a shaman. This is intolerable. It will come down to a choice. Touch the Sky or me."

"There is great anger now over these worthless trade goods," Swift Canoe said. "If it came to a choice now, the headmen would vote for you."

"At any rate," Wolf Who Hunts Smiling said, "the choice will soon be forced upon them. And when it is, White Man Runs Him will not be able to hide behind the Star Chamber. The time rapidly approaches when his guts will string our new bows."

Chapter Twelve

There were five of them squeezed into the cavern.

Touch the Sky, Little Horse, Jack Morningstar, and the burly blacksmith named Captain Bill sat around a new fire in the pit. The cobbler, Otto, sat in the tunnel entrance keeping watch. The Cherokees had again borrowed horses from the work corral. Now they were picketed out of sight with the Cheyenne ponies.

With a 1,000-dollar bounty on the Cheyennes' scalps, all agreed it was safer to take the meeting to them. Little Horse filled his favorite clay pipe with a mixture of tobacco and red willow bark. He knew about the white man's matches; nonetheless, he was thrilled when Captain Bill let him use one to light the pipe. It made the rounds, the fragrant, sweet smell of the bark filling the cave. The Cherokees enjoyed the smoke, but glanced away self-consciously when the two Cheyennes nodded to the four directions of the wind before taking their first puff.

Soon, voices were raised in lively argument.

"I tell you, things are looking better," Captain Bill said. Elation tinged his voice. "The ban on hunting has been lifted. Now we can eat fresh meat without going to jail."

"Bow-and-arrow hunting," Jack Morningstar said. "It's still illegal to own a firearm."

"Well, shit. My osage bow will push an arrow clean through a buff and drop it out on the other side. What? You expect sweet cream and pie, too?"

"This is what makes me mad," Morningstar said. "The white man takes every damn thing we got. Then he gives us some little thing back, and there's always some yack like you to call him generous for it. My old man owned a rifle, and his old man before him. And they didn't bow down to no white man to get 'em."

"It's not just hunting," Otto said from the cave entrance. He couldn't see the others, but he could hear them. "Don't forget that. Long says he's going to drop the tithing system, too. No more making one man suffer for the crimes of ten."

"Ahuh," Morningstar said. "You just wait. Mankiller will still have his spies and informers planted."

Despite the vigorous debate ensuing, a strong bond of camaraderie linked these five. They were fighting back, and already there were encouraging signs. Touch the Sky and Little Horse deliberately held back, letting the Cherokees work this out. In one sense it was every red man's battle, and they were all in it as one. But this was the Cherokee homeland now, and they would have to live with the consequences of whatever decisions they reached in this fight.

"And don't forget," Morningstar said, "Long ain't said word one about our allotments. That flour we been getting, with the weevils in it. The Mexican-grade coffee that tastes like a cup of warm gun oil. Where's the church we was supposed to get? Money was sent from back east for lumber and nails. I ain't seen no building go up."

Touch the Sky translated for Little Horse. This was the crucial point, so far as helping their own tribe up in the Powder Country. Not until the Cherokees set a legal precedent against Steele could Caleb Riley and the Cheyennes also try to seek justice through the hair-face courts. Secretly, Touch the Sky hoped Steele would back down before it came to that. Making good on his promises would benefit both tribes. It would also spare undue suffering for Kristen.

"I'm not forgetting all that," Captain Bill said. "And I ain't never forgetting your wife and all the rest who died because Long and Steele stole the money sent for medicine."

A long silence greeted this remark. Morningstar finished his cigarette and flicked it down into the firepit.

"The thing of it is," he said, "Long has

promised that things're gonna get better. Good. Touch the Sky and Little Horse put the fear of God in the greedy bastard! He's a coward at heart, and I think we can keep him on the straight and narrow just by refusing to take shit from him.

"Steele—I don't know how to call it with him. I'd wager he's no coward in a fight, but he's practical about money. I think he might fold if we make the stakes too expensive. But Mankiller? I can tell you right now. He don't have any boss, neither Steele nor Long and sure's hell not Red Jacket. He makes his own law. It's a hard truth, but we'll have to take him and his police on in battle before it's over."

"Friend, you're a few bricks short of a load," Otto said from the tunnel. "How do we do that without rifles? Bows ain't got the range against carbines. The only weapons're all kept located at police headquarters."

"There're other rifles on the reservation," Touch the Sky said quietly. They all looked at him. It was the first he had spoken in some time.

"Long's house," he said. "He's got a little armory in a room downstairs. I saw it. Fifteen, maybe twenty army-issue carbines, locked in racks."

Morningstar nodded. "Sure. That makes sense. Long wouldn't know what to do with 'em. But the white leaders in Washington would insist on having them there. Well, Long has tripled the guard since Little Horse busted his head open for him. So let's talk about how we plan to get those weapons."

*   *   *

Mankiller moved with stealthy precision in the gathering darkness, a smile tugging his lips apart.

The two Cheyennes were crafty at covering their sign. But not so the Cherokees. And now he had finally found the hidden camp. He crouched behind a fallen log, peering out at the dim figure in the entrance of the tunnel. Otto, he finally decided.

Mankiller knew from the sign he'd read that there were too many to attack now. As badly as his fingers itched to count that gold, he couldn't squander the opportunity to kill those Cheyennes. They were too wily and battle savvy to kill easily in a classic assault.

They would have to be captured another way, according to the ancient laws of the hunt. As for the turncoat Cherokees siding with them—their identities would all be known before the moon above had retired from the sky.

Mankiller slid the Remington from his sash and settled in for a long wait.

"I beg your pardon?" Kristen said.

Hiram Steele said, "Beg all you want, girl. Just do what I said."

"Just like that? You just throw open my door and tell me to pack up everything I own because I'm moving back east?"

"That's the long and the short of it. Your Aunt Thelma can have a go at civilizing you. I give it up for a bad job. You leave on the Tuesday stage out of Nekoma."

140

"That's insane. You're insane!"

"Don't you take that high-hat tone with me, missy! You act so surprised. Hell, I told you before I ain't running no school for genteel society ladies. You got to pull your own freight. I tried to help you get a career, but you just mean mouthed the idea about teaching at the reservation school.

"You had a chance to marry Seth Carlson, but no, you had to play the big muckety-muck and look down your nose at him because he was a soldier."

"Not because he was a soldier. Because of the kind of soldier he was. A mean-spirited, Indian-hating bully."

Hiram snorted. "Huh! That's rich! You're a good one to talk about Indian haters. What the hell you expect a soldier to do with redskins? Wine 'em and dine 'em? Maybe it galled Carlson like it galled me to know you were kissing Matthew Hanchon, and him a Cheyenne. You can't get much lower than to forsake your own Christian race for heathens that run naked."

"Oh, yes, you can," she said. "Lots lower. You and Ephraim Long proved that."

For a moment, rage mottled his face purple. He doubled both fists until the knuckles turned white. Kristen shrank back from him, sure he would hit her.

But he got control of himself as he thought of something else. A smug smile settled on his face. His calm voice, when he spoke now, was more chilling to her than his enraged shouting.

"Go downstairs," he told her. "I left something for you on the dining room table. A little surprise."

She hesitated, not liking his manner.

"Go ahead," he urged her. "Go see what it is. You'll understand things better."

A cold sense of doom accompanied her down the steps. She reached the bottom, opened the door, and glanced into the dining room with her heart thumping hard.

At first she saw nothing on the table. Then she saw what he must mean, but for a moment she didn't understand. Why was there a broken shingle at the place where she usually sat? What could it possibly—A broken shingle!

Cold blood surged into her face, and she whirled to confront her grinning father. He stood a few steps above her.

"Recognize it?" he said softly.

"I don't know what you—" She faltered, her voice failing her.

"I found that in the yard," he said. "Right under your window. Funny thing. And it didn't just fall off. You can see where the nail was bent when somebody put weight on it."

"I don't understand. I—"

"You had that pagan bastard in your bedroom!" he said, his voice heavy with urgent disgust.

She was dizzy, the floor swayed under her like the deck of a storm-tossed ship. "No! I—"

"That loud thump I heard the other night, when you said you dropped something." His face twisted in disgust as he looked at her.

"That was your bed breaking, wasn't it, when that savage topped you?"

Despite the obvious accusation, the enormity of this charge made it impossible to comprehend his meaning. When she finally realized what he was suggesting, anger rose up out of her like a tight bubble escaping. Her only impulse now was to lash back in kind.

"The bed breaking? But, Pa, he's an animal, remember? He took me on the floor."

He slapped her so hard that the sound reverberated all the way up the stairwell.

"You whore," he said gruffly. "A daughter of mine, rutting with wild savages. The only thing keeps me from telling the world and shaming you is that it would shame me even more. But, by God, I will get you out from under my roof. You—"

But stifling a sob, she rushed past him and returned to her room. The door banged shut, and Steele could hear her giving vent to her tears in earnest.

Despite his deep mistrust of his daughter, Steele knew damn well Kristen hadn't done the thing he'd accused her of. Just as he didn't really plan to send her packing next Tuesday. He had no intention of hiring a cook and maid when he had one living there already. And soon he could collect a teacher's salary in her name and reinvest that money to make more.

No, the ruse with sending her back to Thelma's was a gamble. He was sure that she would somehow get word to Hanchon, just as sure that Hanchon would try to see her before she

143

left. Steele had already hired a man to watch the house by night, to follow Kristen anytime she left the house. He planned to give his daughter plenty of freedom of movement between now and Tuesday. Enough rope to hang herself— and Matthew Hanchon.

Chapter Thirteen

There was only one reasonably strong, fast horse in the common corral. And a raid on Long's house would require fast mounts since it was located in open terrain. So it was decided that only three would assault the armory: Touch the Sky, Little Horse, and Jack Morningstar.

They chose the day the white man's winter-count called Monday—a day, according to Morningstar, that Ephraim Long always spent in the hair-face settlement of Great Bend. The three friends agreed the armed guards would be less vigilant with Long absent. For this same reason they decided on a broad-daylight strike, when it would be least expected.

Morningstar had little experience with fire-arms, but he was a fair hand with a bow. For this raid he would carry the Spencer carbine taken from the Cherokee guard at Long's house. But he also fashioned a new bow. Touch the Sky and Little Horse exchanged long, silent looks of approval when the Cherokee carved the battle totems of his clan into the bow. He gratefully accepted several of the Cheyennes' light, flint-tipped arrows and slid them into his tow quiver.

From the crossed-stick shelves at the back of his cabin, the Cherokee took a chamois drawstring pouch. He stuffed it into his hip pocket, instead of tying it to his belt. But both Cheyennes realized it was the personal medicine carried into combat by every Cherokee warrior. No one ever saw it but the warrior or the enemy who vanquished him.

"My father's," he said self-consciously, seeing them watch him. "Ain't been off that shelf in a long time."

For these two battle-scarred Cheyennes, who faced combat or the threat of combat constantly, they were riding out on an all-too-familiar mission. For them, fighting esprit and gallant actions had become a common virtue of survival. For the Cherokee, however, this was a belated rite of passage, a test of his courage and warrior skill—a test he had not passed as had his comrades. Touch the Sky and Little Horse knew this, and they felt the extra measure of respect warriors feel for men who, though frightened and inexperienced, faced the fight bravely.

They rode boldly out from Morningstar's cabin, not worrying about who saw them in the blazing noon sun. They rode three abreast, the two Cheyennes on sturdy mustangs. Morningstar rode a dark cream with black mane and tail—slightly swayback, but strong and sure-footed and quick for short bursts.

All three mounts were battle rigged. Lances, axes, all their weapons secured with ropes where they would be quick to hand. Touch the Sky rode with the butt plate of his heavy Sharps resting against his thigh, the muzzle pointing straight up. He scanned the land all around them, alert for any movement. They spotted a few Cherokees working in the fields or walking along the dirt roads. Some of them waved to this menacing trio of riders. Most, however, stared in astonishment before running off to tell somebody the news.

But they encountered none of Mankiller's deputies. They already knew there were three guards protecting the house. As they topped a long rise, the central clearing rose into view below. Long's house sat on the far side of the big, open meadow.

"There," Touch the Sky said. "See them? Two in the front, one in the back."

"How should we take the fight to them, brother?" Little Horse said, gazing around them. From here to the house there was not enough cover to hide a rabbit.

"Straight and fast," Touch the Sky said, his mouth a grim, determined slit. "Let these fat policemen meet the pony warriors from the Powder Country. Morningstar! Watch us and do as we do—unless you see us get killed," he added, a reckless grin suddenly splitting his face, and his surprised comrades both laughed out loud at his humor.

Touch the Sky raised his rifle high overhead and unleashed the shrill, yipping Cheyenne war cry: "Hi-ya, hii-ya!"

All three Indians urged their mounts to a gallop. As they rode they fanned out in a skirmish line. When their ponies approached the maximum effective range of the Cherokee carbines, Touch the Sky and Little Horse went into the classic Cheyenne riding position for battle. They slid far forward and down on the ponies' necks, reducing the target for their enemies. Morningstar emulated them, though less agilely.

The two Cherokees in the front yard had been playing checkers, the board on the grass between them. They seemed unsure, at first, that they were indeed being attacked. Then one of them shouted to their companion out back, and he joined them in front of the house.

The guards decided to rely on the open country as the best defense. All three Cherokees went into the prone position, digging an elbow into the ground and locking their weapons into their shoulders. They opened fire in earnest when the attackers were perhaps 300 yards out.

Cheyennes never wasted ammunition to make noise, as the Comanches and Kiowas liked to do. So Little Horse was saving his shotgun for close range. Now, aiming from under his horse's neck, he strung an arrow from a fistful in his right hand.

One deputy rose to change his position, and

three arrows raced toward him in as many
eyeblinks. The first two zipped wide. The
third thumped into the deputy's chest so
hard it pushed pink lung tissue in a stream
out his back.

Touch the Sky drew a bead on the middle
deputy and fired, the big Sharps kicking into his
shoulder socket. The shot missed. He dropped
the rifle into its boot and urged his mustang
forward even as he drew his ax from the rigging.
His Cherokee target was desperately thumbing
cartridges into the loading gate when Touch the
Sky threw the ax. It twirled in midair, sliced into
his enemy's head, and opened his skull to expose
bloody curds of brain matter.

The third deputy hit Morningstar's horse in its
vitals, dropping it stone dead. Jack hit the ground
hard, lost his carbine, rolled several times, then
came up on his feet with an arrow strung in his
bow. His string sang out and the arrow caught
the remaining deputy in the left eye. He lay in
the grass, screaming piteously, his legs flailing
until he turned his own weapon on himself
and fired.

And with that final shot of self-destruction, the
battle was over. The acrid smell of spent cordite
hung thick in the air; the Cherokee ponies were
still rearing in fright at all the commotion. And
three men lay dead in the yard, their blood
staining the grass.

"This place hears me!" Touch the Sky declared,
looking at Morningstar. "I take no joy in the
death of these Cherokees. Their wives are wid-
ows now; their children have no father. I would

gladly smear charcoal on my face to celebrate after killing a Pawnee. But these deaths here only leave me sad that these red men played the Indian turncoat for whiteskins."

The armory was located at the rear of the house on the ground floor, in a room which also doubled as Long's private library. The carbines were locked in wooden racks behind a heavy iron lock and chain. But the three Indians used fireplace pokers to snap the chain. They stowed the Spencers in gunny sacks provided by Morningstar. They also cleaned out the stores of powder and lead.

They left the dead in the front yard for Long to discover upon his return, grim and final notice that this fight was going all the way. The Cherokees could arm themselves for the inevitable battle with Mankiller's Indian hard cases.

However, Touch the Sky's elation was short-lived. That night he sneaked into the settlement of Great Bend. Under cover of a cloud-banked sky, he checked for messages from Kristen under the pile of bricks in the Steeles' back yard.

He found one. And it told him that tomorrow she was being sent away forever.

Kristen had also warned Touch the Sky in her note not to come around the house anymore because her father had found out they were meeting. But the knowledge that she was leaving for good forced Touch the Sky to admit that he wanted to see her. Once they had loved each other so much. And when that love was suddenly made impossible by her father's hatred, it left a permanent ache like an important promise left unfulfilled.

Touch the Sky knew in his heart that his love belonged to Honey Eater, that his place was with the Cheyenne people. But Kristen held a special place, too, especially since she had suffered greatly for her loyalty to him and for her steadfast concern for the red man. Hadn't Jack Morningstar, to whom bitterness and cynicism were no strangers, praised Kristen's kindness toward his dying wife? If Steele was punishing her like this, Touch the Sky had to at least find out if anything could possibly be done for her.

Touch the Sky crouched in the shadow of the rickety storage shed, unsure what to do as he looked toward the house. Kristen's window was aglow with lamplight, though he saw no sign of her.

What to do? How close, he wondered, was Hiram watching her? And then he started to worry. What if Steele, whose dangerous rage could rival Black Elk's, had hurt his daughter?

Touch the Sky made up his mind. He had to take a chance and find out.

He glanced carefully around the shadow-mottled yard and slipped up to one back corner of the house. He shot quickly up to the front of the house and looked across the street. A bored-looking man in a floppy-brim hat stood in the shadows, smoking a cigarette and watching the house.

But Touch the Sky felt little threat from the man. The Cheyenne stuck close to the house and made his way back to Kristen's window. He fished for a pebble and tossed it up. It clinked against the glass. He waited, but there was no sign of Kristen.

He tossed another pebble, and another. Perhaps she wasn't in her room. He arched his neck and saw that the sash was open a few inches. It would be a great risk, but he could go up and wait for her.

Again he moved to the front of the house and checked on the guard across the street. The man had knelt out of the wind to build himself another cigarette. Touch the Sky dismissed him as a threat and returned to the window.

Another pebble. No response.

His shaman sense was back, a vague tingling deep in his bones. It warned of trouble, but that same sense told him to face the trouble, that it might be like the crisis stage of a fever and best put behind him.

He gripped the lightning rod and pulled himself up hand over hand. He reached the sill, then peeked over. The room appeared empty. Touch the Sky slid the sash up wider and hauled himself over the sill.

The vague tingling in his bones became a cold, numb certainty in his skin. He looked to his right and stared into the twin bores of a scattergun.

"Welcome to the Steele residence," Hiram Steele said. "Most people wait until they're invited."

The fear Touch the Sky felt upon spotting the weapon now gave way to a cold contempt. This frontier bully had driven the Cheyenne's adopted white parents out of the mercantile business and had tried to destroy their mustang ranch as well.

"Kristen couldn't be here to entertain you," Steele said. "She sends her regrets."

Steele's scornful laugh was brash and loud. His man outside had watched Kristen hide her note for the Cheyenne. Steele had read it, then left it there, guessing it would lure the Indian. He had guessed right.

"You're a dead man, you son of a bitch," Steele said. "Do you realize you just broke into a white man's house? Ain't no court in the country will try a white man for killing a blanket Indian who broke into his house, especially his daughter's bedroom."

"You're a coward, Steele. A criminal coward. You hire out thugs to do your dirty work, like these Cherokee hard cases you arm to terrorize the reservation. But it doesn't matter now if you kill me. It's too late. Three of your hired guns are already dead, and we just got every last weapon out of Long's armory. Your policemen are soon going to be doing the hurt dance. And after they're planted, you and Long are next."

Steele had turned pale when Touch the Sky mentioned the weapons. "You're a liar! A stinking, flea-bitten liar."

Touch the Sky laughed in his face. "Am I? Go ahead and kill me. But stand by for a blast if you do because my friend Little Horse is waiting for me to return. When the moccasin telegraph tells him you killed me, you won't find one place to hide from him. You remember Little Horse, Steele? He sent quite a few of your thugs across the Great Divide. And he's been waiting for a piece of your scalp—especially now that you've robbed our tribe with that shipment of shoddy trash."

"It's all he-bear talk," Steele said.

But Touch the Sky read the doubt in the man's cold, hard, flint-gray eyes. Now, thought Touch the Sky. It was time to act.

"And before you pull those triggers, Steele, let me ask you something. Do you remember a time when you wrote a certain letter to your partner Long? A letter you spilled ink all over and never posted? Maybe you were a little drunk when you wrote it. Maybe that's why you mentioned so many incriminating details of your illegal operations. Maybe that's also why you decided not to send it. You sure's hell said a lot of things in that letter, things that would get your ass skinned in the white-man's court. And, Steele, you signed it. It's got your wax seal on it."

Steele's face clouded. He didn't quite understand what this brazen young buck was driving at.

Now Touch the Sky shot his bolt. He quoted a line that he remembered from reading the letter so many times. " 'This Great Bend Reservation is our nut to crack, Long. We'll get rich off these godless savages and let the Indian lovers in Congress take the heat for it.' "

These words jogged Steele's memory, and blood rushed into his face.

"I came into your house a while back and found that letter," Touch the Sky lied. "Little Horse has it now. If anything happens to me, he will take it to our cavalry friend Tom Riley. Riley hates you with a strong passion. He'll make it the mission of his life to see you burn.

"The same thing happens if you do one damn thing to hurt Kristen for this. I swear it! She'll be getting out from under your roof as soon as she can anyway. You just leave her be."

Steele's face showed he was defeated, though he still held the gun on Touch the Sky. On the frontier, men winked at those who swindled Indians. Back east, however, the newspapers railed against such activities. If he was ever named by a prominent writer, the Indian Bureau would drop him like a bad habit. Even worse, some men became public examples and were harshly prosecuted. He could even be ordered to pay all his illegal profits back.

The Cheyenne watched all this play on Steele's face. He backed to the window and lowered himself down, expecting a load of buckshot to tear off his face at any moment.

Instead, he slipped off into the black folds of night. Elation tingled in his blood. The immediate threat from Long or Steele was effectively hobbled. However, the Cheyenne also cursed his own carelessness. He had lied about giving the letter to Little Horse; he had had it with him all along. Had Steele thought to search him, Touch the Sky would be dead by now.

As he made his way closer to Pawnee Creek and his hobbled pony, Jack Morningstar's words reverberated inside his skull. *Mankiller makes his own law. We'll have to take him and his police on in battle before it's over.*

Chapter Fourteen

Armed now for a fair fight, the Cherokees none-theless tried the peace road one last time.

Morningstar and some of the other skilled tradesmen had formed a temporary council of headmen. They ousted Red Jacket as chief and voted to send a message to Long, Steele, Mankiller, and Red Jacket to surrender, nego-tiate in good faith for change, and all future bloodshed could be avoided.

Red Jacket, a wily survivor who changed politics with the wind, immediately capitu-lated in a statement about his love for Indian self-determination. Long, too, was in favor of appeasement. However, it was Hiram Steele and Mankiller who prevailed. And neither man was willing to negotiate a point. For by now Steele had thought it all over and realized that the incriminating letter could never be turned over if both Cheyennes were killed, for one of them was carrying it. Only if they left this place alive could that letter be used against him.

At Steele's insistence, Long wired an emergency request for troops from Fort Hays, citing an armed uprising by hostile Indians. Mankiller and his deputies, in the meantime, turned their reinforced police headquarters into a bastion. Food, water, and ammunition were stockpiled. Their plan was to wait there for the pony soldiers to arrive from Fort Hays, then lead the fight to disarm the rebels.

But Touch the Sky and his comrades knew—thanks to the moccasin telegraph—about the request for troops. And thus they also knew they had to move first before they arrived. Surrounding the police and holding them would not be enough. They would be safe once the army arrived. And they could not be left in a position to ever again terrorize the reservation. The Cherokee council had agreed on this point unanimously.

The decision was unpleasant but also unavoidable. A bloody battle loomed.

Touch the Sky and Little Horse studied the police headquarters, a long, low building made of thick cottonwood logs and loopholed for rifles. Its site had been chosen with the thought of armed rebellion in mind. It was located on high ground, a lone rise in the middle of a vast expanse of open grass. At one end of the building, hunkering on the least exposed flank, was a smaller, windowless stone building with a heavy iron lock on the door.

This, Morningstar explained, was the main powder cache for the reservation.

"A lot more in there than we got from Long's place," he said. The three friends were hidden in a tree line at the bottom of the rise, getting the lay of the land.

Touch the Sky and Little Horse traded uneasy glances. This was not a promising scenario for a battle. That rise was steep, by plains standards, and anyone riding or running up toward the headquarters would be a low, easy, dangerously vulnerable target. Morningstar estimated that as many as 17 or 18 braves were holed up there— a formidable fighting force, especially on high ground.

"We will need a diversion," Touch the Sky said.

"What type of diversion?" Morningstar asked.

Touch the Sky shook his head, still unsure on that point.

"Something," he insisted, "or the battle will be a slaughter, and we will be the slaughtered."

Time was critical. Troops at Fort Hays were combat ready and could be dispatched immediately. Within three sleeps, Touch the Sky knew, the reservation would be swarming with bluecoats. The place had to be ready for them, with the real criminals out of power and a new system in place. This final battle had to also break Steele and Long.

The new council met in the skilled tradesmen's lodge to select men for the raid. The building overflowed with volunteers. Only braves with 18 winters or more behind them were selected. The warriors were issued weapons and divided into battle groups. Because Touch the Sky, Little Horse, Jack Morningstar, Captain Bill, and Otto had already ridden on one mission together, they would form the spearhead group. Due to the steep rise, this would not be a mounted battle— a good thing, since sound horses were scarce.

The confrontation was set to begin at sunrise. Braves broke into their battle groups to make sure each warrior understood how to crimp a cartridge in a carbine and prime the seven-shot cylinder. Old men who had fought in the Creek Wars back east, or against whiteskins, took the young warriors aside to share advice with them.

"Brother," Little Horse said, the lodge buzzing all around them, "have you given more thought to this diversion you mentioned?"

"I have, brother."

Touch the Sky caught Jack Morningstar's attention and waved him over. "How much black powder do we have?"

"Not so much. Enough to ration out maybe eight or ten shots per man."

Touch the Sky nodded. He handed Morningstar a chamois pouch. "Put out the word. Every brave going into battle is to measure out one hundred grains of powder—enough for one shot. Each is to put it in this pouch."

By now Morningstar's respect for the Cheyennes was complete. He accepted the pouch.

"Sure I'll do it," he said. "But what's it for?"

"A diversion," Touch the Sky said evasively, adding a nervy little smile.

An hour before sunrise, the attackers gathered in a cedar copse well below the police headquarters. The rise could be seen even in the predawn gloom, a huge, black mass against the lighter gray of the sky.

Touch the Sky and his group moved among the warriors, calming the younger and more nervous ones, checking weapons and equipment. Again and again, Morningstar and the other Cherokee leaders repeated a Sioux battle slogan adopted by the Cheyenne: *One bullet, one enemy.*

"Here," Morningstar said, handing Touch the Sky the pouch, now puffy from the load of black powder within. "What do you plan on doing with it?"

"Keep your eyes open, Cherokee, and you'll find out."

Little Horse knew his friend well, and he had already guessed what Touch the Sky had in mind. His guess was confirmed when he saw Touch the Sky, in the light of a small fire, fashioning several exploding arrows. These crude explosives, a Cheyenne invention, were made by tying a primer cap to the edge of an arrow point. Then a little pouch filled with gunpowder was tied over the arrow point. With luck, on impact the primer cap would ignite the powder, causing a small explosion and sometimes a fire. They were good detonators for larger explosives. Touch the Sky and Little Horse had used them before with varying success. They did not always work.

For this reason, he handed Little Horse three exploding arrows.

"Place these in your quiver, brother, and guard them closely. When I tie this pouch of powder to the door of that armory, wait for me to clear out. Then shoot the pouch with an exploding arrow. With luck, that will set off the powder inside."

Little Horse didn't like this plan. For one thing, Touch the Sky would have to wait until daylight before he covered that open, uphill expanse on foot. Otherwise, Little Horse could not see to shoot it right away. And if not detonated immediately, it would be discovered and removed.

"Buck," Little Horse said, "you always claim the best sport for yourself. Let me run that powder up the hill."

Touch the Sky shook his head. Little Horse had been permanently slowed down when his right kneecap was shattered aboard the land-grabber Wes Munro's keelboat. Now he walked with a distinct limp.

"You are a better shot than I with a bow, brother."

This was true and Little Horse fell silent. The battle plan was repeated one final time for all the warriors. First would come a heavy barrage of fire arrows. These would force some of the policemen outside to quell the flames. Then the Cherokees below were to fire only carefully timed staggered volleys—one battle group at a time to conserve ammunition.

It was during this stage, while their enemies

were distracted by the fire arrows, that Touch the Sky would make his run for the door of the armory. If they succeeded in blowing it and detonating the powder within, a massed charge was to occur close on the heels of the explosion.

If they couldn't blow up that armory, Touch the Sky knew the battle might still be won. But the price would be bloody; that hill would be littered with dead Cherokees—and perhaps a pair of Cheyennes.

It was Jack Morningstar, the Acting Chief of the Cherokee Nation, who spoke the final words.

"The men on top that hill know they face hard justice if they surrender. So don't expect them to. They've murdered and beaten too many of us, stolen too much from us. It's going to be a fierce and bloody battle."

Then he surprised Touch the Sky by shouting out, "Cowards to the rear!"

It was an old Cherokee battle ritual to inspire courage in the final moment before battle. The two visiting Cheyennes were visibly impressed when, to the last man, the Cherokees raised their weapons at the ready and took two steps forward.

Their sister the sun abruptly set the eastern sky on fire. With each battle group in position, the first fire arrows were unleashed.

They flew through the pale gray light and thwacked hard into the cottonwood building. Soon the building was bright with tiny fires. Green cottonwood did not catch fire easily, yet once it did, it flared up quickly. One or two of the fires were serious enough to draw a few policemen outside.

Mankiller's deputies suffered no lack of ammunition. While the men were sent outside to smother the flames, at least a dozen rifles spat muzzle fire out the loopholed wall.

A deadly hail of bullets shot through the trees all around the attackers. Touch the Sky heard a Cherokee attacker cry out as he was wounded. But the Cheyenne was busy working his way around to the far side of the rise. He made sure Little Horse was in place, exploding arrows at the ready.

Then, while the second battle group opened up with covering fire, Touch the Sky raised his Sharps in front of his chest at a high port. He broke from cover and began the longest run of his life.

At first his heart swelled with surprised elation as he realized he was drawing no fire! Perhaps all the defenders were distracted to the front.

But then someone must have spotted him. For a heartbeat later—about one-third way up the hill—he ran into a deadly hail of lead.

Dirt fountained up from the ground all around his feet, bullets buzzed past his ears so close they sounded like angry hornets. He cut to the left, feinted hard right, and zigzagged in a crazy pattern so he wasn't easy to draw a bead on. But the closer he got, the more intense the fire he drew. A bullet grazed his left arm so close that it cut through the protective band of leather around his wrist; another creased his inner thigh and left a blood gutter. But screaming a defiant war cry, he finally hit the top and dived headlong for the shelter of the little stone armory.

Now he worked quickly, knowing time was the key. If he hugged the armory close and stayed on the west side, he couldn't easily be hit from the building nearby. He had nearly tied the pouch of black powder into place when the door of the police barracks banged open and two men darted out.

Touch the Sky picked up his Sharps, hit the ground rolling, came up, and snapped off a round. It punched into one deputy's chest and slammed him back inside. The second fired at Touch the Sky and missed, then levered his carbine and fired again. Below, Little Horse—armed with a carbine—broke out from behind cover and fired. The second policeman sprawled in the dirt, blood blossoming from his skull.

Touch the Sky finished securing the pouch, then frantically signaled to Little Horse. He didn't waste time running. He simply leaped downhill from the doorway and then rolled hard to get out of blast range.

Desperately, reloading his Sharps and covering that barracks door, he watched Little Horse string his bow below. The first exploding arrow had good range and detonated properly. But unfortunately it missed the pouch by inches. The little fire it started went out quickly.

Steady brother, Touch the Sky thought as Little Horse aimed his second arrow. It was a powerful shot and struck the pouch, but the primer failed to detonate.

One arrow left. Little Horse aimed and fired. The arrow thumped into the chamois pouch, and an eyeblink later the pouch exploded. Only a few moments later, the stores inside ignited and a huge fireball flashed up from the hill. Giant chunks of rock flew like cannonballs; the police headquarters lost half of its roof, most of one wall. Screams filled the interior.

Shouting battle cries, the Cherokees below began their assault. But the battle was over. The policemen staggering out of the building, many bloody or burned, were throwing down their weapons and waving white cloths in surrender.

Touch the Sky covered them while his companions raced to join him. But though he anxiously studied the faces of the emerging survivors, the one he hoped to see most never appeared.

Dead, maybe?

Then, below, Captain Bill shouted and pointed to the far side of the hill. Touch the Sky looked where he pointed and saw a huge bear of a man just then disappearing into the trees. Somehow, in the chaos of the battle, the wily Mankiller had made his escape.

By the time the troops arrived from Fort Hays, they found the Great Bend Cherokee Reservation all secure from the top down.

As Touch the Sky had predicted, this final show of strength had taken all the fight out of Ephraim Long—a man with no stomach for hard fighting. He resigned his position, effective upon the arrival of a new, reform-minded agent selected by the Quakers instead of the Indian Bureau.

The new Cherokee council sentenced the crooked Red Chief to permanent banishment from the Cherokee Nation. Jack Morningstar accepted the position of permanent tribal chief. And most important, the dreaded police force was disbanded in favor of a more honest system of unarmed constables and an all-Indian court.

Hiram Steele was badly frightened by this sudden and drastic turn of events on the reservation. With his ally Long out of the picture, he began to worry anew about that incriminating letter in Matthew Hanchon's possession. He began hasty deliveries of long-overdue goods—serviceable goods this time, not the shoddy substitutes.

But he also sent word to the two Cheyennes, an especially welcome message. He had already made arrangements to make restitution to the Cheyenne people, too. The pack train would be on its way to the Powder River camp within the next few days.

Still, Touch the Sky knew better than to celebrate this as yet another victory. For among the former policemen now serving time in the reservation jail, one face was missing.

Both Cheyennes knew that Mankiller was still out there somewhere, waiting to kill them.

Chapter Fifteen

Triumphant, but tired, Touch the Sky and Little Horse made their final ride to the hidden camp on Pawnee Creek.

For the assault on the police building, they had brought only their weapons. Now they were returning to pack their sleeping robes and other gear for the long ride back to their own hunting grounds.

"You heard Morningstar, brother," Little Horse said. "The hair-face businessmen promise that our tribe's contract goods will be on their way by the time we reach camp. Do you believe this thing?"

Touch the Sky thought about it, then nodded. "This time, yes. I am not fool enough to believe Hiram Steele has felt a change in his heart. Only, he looks to his past and knows the hair-face soldiers already have his name in their books as a troublemaker. Thanks to Tom Riley, he was investigated in Bighorn Falls. He is doing this now only because he fears to lose money.

"Count upon it, buck. When the sting from his present fear wears off, he will prowl his usual grounds. We have not seen the last of him or his insane greed."

"Straight words, Cheyenne. But at least for now the Cherokees are no longer eating putrid meat."

The question nagging at both bucks was so constant, neither had to voice it. Where was Mankiller? Had he done the wise thing and left the reservation for good?

Neither Cheyenne believed that. Mankiller was not one who lived for the wise choice. He was very much like Hiram Steele in one respect. He could not brook defeat, and these two Cheyennes had so far defeated him.

For this reason, they approached the cave with even more caution than usual. First they studied the area from the tops of tall cottonwoods before they even neared the dense thicket that covered the entrance to the cave. As they approached, leading their ponies at a walk, they stopped again and again so sharp-eared Little Horse could listen closely.

Touch the Sky watched his calico mustang closely, alert for any signs of nervousness. Likewise, he studied the birds in the area for the briefest signs of alarm. His eyes swept the surrounding growth, scoured the ground, and constantly watched their back trail.

Mankiller

Nothing amiss. Nothing. Yet every nerve in his body felt the death chill on it.

For the final approach they maintained absolute silence, communicating only with signs. Employing a scouting trick Black Elk had taught them, the two braves stood back to back and revolved slowly, thus double scanning the terrain.

Still nothing amiss. They hobbled their ponies. Little Horse held his scattergun close, all four revolving barrels loaded. Knowing his rifle was clumsy at close range, Touch the Sky had opted for his knife. He held it in his right hand, low and close to his side. If forced to use it, he would stab low and upward, the hardest thrust to block.

They dropped to a crouch, approached on hands and knees at intervals of about six feet. Still nothing amiss. They were so quiet that two squirrels playing near the cave entrance still hadn't heard them.

The Cheyennes exchanged a glance. If squirrels were playing that close and a thrush was singing on a branch just above the cave, Mankiller mustn't be near.

Little Horse nodded, some of the tension easing from his face.

A moment later, fear caught them by the throat and they glimpsed the face of the Wendigo. Little Horse had veered slightly left to avoid a muddy swale. Abruptly, a powerful grip enveloped his left arm and he was jerked right up off the ground—up into the treetops. It happened in an eyeblink, the sapling snare was tripped when his hand came down.

Not only did the sudden, powerful snap of the tree unbending pull Little Horse's shoulder painfully out of socket, it made him drop his shotgun. If their plight had not been utterly desperate, he would have looked comical dangling so far off the ground, legs flailing.

But their plight was desperate, for those squirrels at play meant nothing. The moment Little Horse was jerked up from the ground, Mankiller lunged from the cave and leaped on Touch the Sky.

It was too quick to comprehend. Touch the Sky still hadn't grasped what was happening to Little Horse. Now the air was thumped from his chest and he was driven back hard by Mankiller's weight and sudden, jarring kick to the back as he whammed into a tree. The double impact, front and back, was like being caught in the cross kick of two powerful mules. Touch the Sky saw a bright orange burst inside his skull; then his world was nothing but pain.

Touch the Sky had dropped his knife when he was slammed into the tree. Now, his eyes big and bright with eager triumph, Mankiller circled his victim's neck with those huge, powerful hands.

Touch the Sky's head, too, had knocked hard into the tree. He teetered on the brink of awareness—enough consciousness left to be aware that, incredibly, his body was suffering even more pain.

Touch the Sky had been choked before, but this was different. The blood flow and air were both stopped immediately, and the viselike power of the grip defied belief. Mankiller, those eyes never once blinking as they bored into him, picked him up off the ground as he throttled him.

Touch the Sky had no strength to fight this bear, though every instinct in his body urged him to struggle to the last breath and beyond. So he did, though his efforts were pathetic and useless. Death was coming for him on incredibly swift wings; the world was closing down to darkness and raw pain.

He had no breath for his death song, but his final thoughts were for Honey Eater and Little Horse and Arrow Keeper, and when Arrow Keeper's face passed before his mind's dying eye, the words from the old shaman's disturbing medicine dream came to Touch the Sky. *Be prepared to die before you are dead.*

And then Touch the Sky understood.

There were a few more heartbeats of struggle and awareness left in him. But instead, he pretended to die. He suddenly slumped heavily and went slack, perfectly feigning death while actually on the threshold.

Mankiller was disappointed, even in his elation. He had expected more of a fight from this formidable-appearing Cheyenne foe. Instead, he turned out to be nearly as fragile as a woman. Perhaps the other one would provide more entertainment.

Mankiller threw the dead Cheyenne down in disgust.

A few eyeblinks later, cold obsidian slid between his fourth and fifth rib and pierced his heart as the supposedly dead Cheyenne leaped up from the ground and stabbed him in one smooth, fluid movement.

Touch the Sky was so weak from his ordeal and the effort that he could not get out of the way when Mankiller's dead body fell on him. For a moment Little Horse was sure both of them were dead. Then he heard his friend roar in disgust as he squirmed out from under their tormentor.

And despite his own incredible pain, Little Horse felt his face go numb with shock when his brother staggered to his feet and looked upward. Already Touch the Sky's neck had swollen so huge it looked like he had no chin.

"Brother," Little Horse said through teeth clenched in pain, "are you alive or a thing of smoke?"

Touch the Sky's voice was weak, but miraculously, still there. "A thing of smoke would not be able to cut you down. You had best not send me over too quickly."

The two friends reported Mankiller's death to Jack Morningstar and requested permission to remain for two more sleeps, recovering enough to make the long ride north and west to the upcountry of the Powder. The grateful Cherokee Council made sure they were well equipped for the journey. Before they rode out, they were also informed that they both had the status of voting headmen for any Cherokee Council meeting— one of the highest honors and marks of friendship an Indian could bestow on a red man from another tribe.

Mankiller

But despite their many important victories, that ride home was difficult for both of them. Because, in their absence, their many enemies had surely been at work against them. Touch the Sky knew important changes loomed. Arrow Keeper lay seriously ill, if not already dead. Black Elk's jealousy had festered so long it was a deadly poison. And the power-hungry Wolf Who Hunts Smiling could not wait much longer before killing the one man who blocked the path of his ambition.

Yes, this fight at Great Bend was behind them, a glorious victory to be proud of. But old Arrow Keeper was right. For a Cheyenne, life meant being a warrior, and the end of one battle marked only the beginning of the next.

CHEYENNE

JUDD COLE

Follow the adventures of Touch the Sky as he searches for a world he can call his own!

#3: Renegade Justice. When his adopted white parents fall victim to a gang of ruthless outlaws, Touch the Sky swears to save them—even if it means losing the trust he has risked his life to win from the Cheyenne.

__3385-2 $3.50 US/$4.50 CAN

#4: Vision Quest. While seeking a mystical sign from the Great Spirit, Touch the Sky is relentlessly pursued by his enemies. But the young brave will battle any peril that stands between him and the vision of his destiny.

__3411-5 $3.50 US/$4.50 CAN

LEISURE BOOKS
ATTN: Order Department
276 5th Avenue, New York, NY 10001

Please add $1.50 for shipping and handling for the first book and $.35 for each book thereafter. PA., N.Y.S. and N.Y.C. residents, please add appropriate sales tax. No cash, stamps, or C.O.D.s. All orders shipped within 6 weeks via postal service book rate. Canadian orders require $2.00 extra postage and must be paid in U.S. dollars through a U.S. banking facility.

Name _____

Address _____

City _____ State _____ Zip _____

I have enclosed $_____in payment for the checked book(s). Payment <u>must</u> accompany all orders.☐ Please send a free catalog.

Judd Cole
Follow the adventures of Touch the Sky as he searches for a world he can call his own!

#5: Blood on the Plains. When one of Touch the Sky's white friends suddenly appears, he brings with him a murderous enemy—the rivermen who employ him are really greedy land-grabbers out to steal the Indian's hunting grounds. If the young brave cannot convince his tribe that they are in danger, the swindlers will soak the ground with innocent blood.

__3441-7 $3.50 US/$4.50 CAN

#6: Comanche Raid. When a band of Comanche attack Touch the Sky's tribe, the silence of the prairie is shattered by the cries of the dead and dying. If Touch the Sky and the Cheyenne braves can't fend off the vicious war party, they will be slaughtered like the mighty beasts of the plains.

__3478-6 $3.50 US/$4.50 CAN

#7: Comancheros. When a notorious slave trader captures their women and children, Touch the Sky and his brother warriors race to save them so their glorious past won't fade into a bleak and hopeless future.

__3496-4 $3.50 US/$4.50 CAN

LEISURE BOOKS
ATTN: Order Department
276 5th Avenue, New York, NY 10001

Please add $1.50 for shipping and handling for the first book and $.35 for each book thereafter. PA., N.Y.S. and N.Y.C. residents, please add appropriate sales tax. No cash, stamps, or C.O.D.s. All orders shipped within 6 weeks via postal service book rate. Canadian orders require $2.00 extra postage and must be paid in U.S. dollars through a U.S. banking facility.

Name _____

Address _____

City _____ State _____ Zip _____

I have enclosed $_____in payment for the checked book(s). Payment <u>must</u> accompany all orders.☐ Please send a free catalog.

SPEND YOUR LEISURE MOMENTS WITH US.

Hundreds of exciting titles to choose from—something for everyone's taste in fine books: breathtaking historical romance, chilling horror, spine-tingling suspense, taut medical thrillers, involving mysteries, action-packed men's adventure and wild Westerns.

SEND FOR A FREE CATALOGUE TODAY!

**Leisure Books
Attn: Order Department
276 5th Avenue, New York, NY 10001**